R. K. NARAYAN has been called the best Indian novelist writing in English today. Two years ago he received from Nehru the Padma Bhushan, the highest Indian literary award. He visits America frequently. Ved Mehta's famous profile of him in *The New Yorker* showed him as a man who has retained his Hindu faith and loyalties yet is very much in tune with the West. *The Vendor of Sweets* is the tenth of his Malgudi novels. Several of them are now in paperbacks, and one, *The Guide,* has been made into a major movie and is also scheduled for the New York stage in a dramatic version by Harvey Breit.

BY *R. K. Narayan:*

The Vendor of Sweets

NEW YORK: THE VIKING PRESS

PUBLISHED IN 1967 BY THE VIKING PRESS, INC.
625 MADISON AVENUE, NEW YORK, N.Y. 10022

*

LIBRARY OF CONGRESS CATALOG CARD NUMBER: 66-23818

*

SET IN JANSON AND WEISS TYPES AND
PRINTED IN U.S.A. BY THE COLONIAL PRESS INC.

M B G

THE VENDOR OF SWEETS

A glossary of the less familiar Indian words will be found on page 183.

Chapter One

"Conquer taste, and you will have conquered the self," said Jagan to his listener, who asked, "Why conquer the self?" Jagan said, "I do not know, but all our sages advise us so."

The listener lost interest in the question; his aim was only to stimulate conversation, while he occupied a low wooden stool next to Jagan's chair. Jagan sat under the framed picture of the goddess Lakshmi hanging on the wall, and offered prayers first thing in the day by reverently placing a string of jasmine on top of the frame; he also lit an incense stick and stuck it in a crevice in the wall. The air was charged with the scent of jasmine and incense, which imperceptibly blended with the fragrance of sweetmeats frying in ghee in the kitchen across the hall.

The listener was a cousin, though how he came to be called so could not be explained, since he claimed cousinhood with many others in the town (total incompatibles, at times), but if challenged he could always overwhelm the sceptic with genealogy. He was a man-about-town and visited many places and houses from morning till night, and invariably every day at about four-thirty he arrived, threw a brief glance and a nod at Jagan, passed straight into the

3

kitchen, and came out ten minutes later wiping his mouth with the end of a towel on his shoulder, commenting, "The sugar situation may need watching. I hear that the government are going to raise the price. Wheat flour is all right today. I gave that supplier a bit of my mind yesterday when I passed Godown Street. Don't ask me what took me there. I have friends and relations all over this city and everyone wants me to attend to this or that. I do not grudge serving others. What is life worth unless we serve and help each other?"

Jagan asked, "Did you try the new sweet the cook experimented with today?"

"Yes, of course; it is tasty."

"Oh, but I think it is only an old recipe in a new shape. All sweetmeats, after all, are the same. Don't you agree?"

"No, sir," said the cousin, "I still see a lot of difference between one sweet and another. I hope I shall not become a yogi and lose the taste for all."

It was then that Jagan pronounced his philosophy, "Conquer taste and you will have conquered the self." They palavered thus for half an hour more, and then Jagan asked, "Do you know what I eat nowadays?"

"Anything new?" asked the cousin.

"I have given up salt since this morning," Jagan said with a glow of triumph. He noted with satisfaction the effect produced by this announcement and expanded his theory. "One must eat only natural salt."

"What is natural salt?" asked the cousin, and added, "the salt that dries up on one's back when one has run a mile in the sun?"

Jagan made a wry face at the coarse reference. He had the outlook of a disembodied soul floating above the grime of this earth. At fifty-five his appearance was slight and elfish, his brown skin was translucent, his brow receded gently into a walnut shade of baldness, and beyond the fringe his hair fell in a couple of speckled waves on his nape. His chin was covered with whitening bristles, as he shaved only at certain intervals, feeling that to view oneself daily in a mirror was an intolerable European habit. He wore a loose jibba over his dhoti, both made of material spun with his own hand; every day he spun for an hour, retained enough yarn for his sartorial requirements (he never possessed more than two sets of clothes at a time), and delivered all the excess in neat bundles to the local hand-loom committee in exchange for cash. Although the cash he thus earned was less than five rupees a month, he felt a sentimental thrill in receiving it, as he had begun the habit when Gandhi visited the town over twenty years ago, and he had been commended for it. He wore a narrow almond-shaped pair of glasses set in a yellowish frame, and peeped at the world over their pale rims. He draped his shoulders in a khaddar shawl with gaudy yellow patterns on it and shod his feet with thick sandals made out of the leather of an animal which had died of old age. Being a follower of Gandhi, he explained, "I do not like to think that a living creature should have its throat cut for the comfort of my feet," and this occasionally involved him in excursions to remote villages where a cow or calf was reported to be dying. When he secured the hide he soaked it in some solution and then turned it over to an old cobbler he knew, who had his little repair-shop under a tree at the Albert Mission compound.

When his son was six years old he was a happy supporter of Jagan's tanning activities in the back veranda of the house, but as he grew older he began to complain of the stench whenever his father brought home leather. Jagan's wife proved even less tolerant, shutting herself in a room and refusing to come out until the tanning ended. Since it was a prolonged process, carried on over several days, one

5

can understand the dislocation into which the household was thrown whenever Jagan attempted to renew his footwear. It was a difficult and hazardous operation. The presence of the leather at home threatened to blast his domestic life; he had to preserve it, in the early stages of tanning, out of his wife's reach in the fuel shed, where there was danger of rats' nibbling it. When she lay dying, she summoned Jagan to come close to her and mumbled something. He could not make out her words, but was harrowed by the thought that probably she was saying, "Throw away the leather." In deference to what was possibly her last wish, he did give to a mission the last bit of leather at home, and felt happy that he was enabling someone else to take to non-violent footwear. Afterwards he just trusted the cobbler at the Albert Mission to supply his rather complicated footwear.

Now his cousin's reference to natural salt upset his delicate balance and he reddened in the face. The cousin, satisfied with the effect he had produced, tried to restore his mood with a pleasing remark, "You have simplified your life so completely, and made yourself absolutely self-dependent, as I was saying to the Cooperative Registrar the other day . . ." This had the desired effect, and Jagan said, "I have discontinued sugar as you know. I find twenty drops of honey in hot water quite adequate, and that is the natural way of taking in the sugar we need."

"You have perfected the art of living on nothing," said the cousin.

Encouraged, Jagan added, "I have given up rice too. I cook a little stone-ground wheat and take it with honey and greens."

"And yet," said the cousin, "I cannot understand why you go on working and earning, taking all this trouble!" He waved his hands in the direction of the sweets displayed on trays at the window, but stopped short of asking why Jagan should expect others to eat sweets and keep him flourishing. He felt he had said enough, and stirred in his seat. Jagan's counting hour was approaching, and the cousin knew that he should move as Jagan did not like his cash to be watched. The time was six, the peak sales were over, and the front-stall boy would be bringing in the collection for the day. At this moment Jagan almost fancied himself a monarch on a throne surveying his people (consisting of the four cooks in the kitchen and the front-stall boy) and accepting their tributes. The throne was a flat-bottomed wooden chair covered with a thin cushion, hoisted on a platform, strategically placed so that he could keep an eye on all sides of his world of confections. The chair was nearly a century old, with shining brass strips on the arms and back and carved legs, especially made by his father when he built his house behind the Lawley Statue. Normally he would not have bothered to design a piece of furniture, as the family always sat on the polished floor, but he had frequent visits from one Mr. Noble, an Englishman, the District Collector, who came for lessons in astrology and found it painful to sit on the floor, and found it even more painful to extricate himself from the sitting posture at the end of the lessons. A signed portrait ripening yellow with time was among the prized possessions dumped in the loft, but at some point in the history of the family the photograph was brought down, the children played with it for a while, and then substituted in its glassed frame the picture of a God and hung it up, while the photograph in the bare mount was tossed about as the children gazed on Mr. Noble's side whiskers and giggled all afternoon. They fanned themselves with it, too, when the summer became too hot; finally it disappeared back to the loft amidst old account books and such other obscure family junk.

Sitting there, Jagan was filled with a sense of fulfilment.

7

On one side he could hear, see, and smell whatever was happening in the kitchen, whence a constant traffic of trays laden with colourful sweetmeats passed on to the front counter. As long as the frying and sizzling noise in the kitchen continued and the trays passed, Jagan noticed nothing, his gaze unflinchingly fixed on the Sanskrit lines in a red-bound copy of the Bhagavad Gita, but if there was the slightest pause in the sizzling, he cried out, without lifting his eyes from the sacred text, "What is happening?" The head cook would give a routine reply, "Nothing," and that would quieten Jagan's mind and enable it to return to the Lord's sayings until again some slackness was noticed at the front stall and he would shout, "Captain! That little girl in the yellow skirt, ask her what she wants. She has been standing there so long!" His shout would alert the counter attendant as well as the watchman at the door, an ex-army man in khaki, who had a tendency to doze off on his deal-wood seat. Or Jagan would cry, "Captain, that beggar should not be seen here except on Fridays. This is not a charity home."

The surroundings were hushed when the master counted his earnings for the day. Although the boy at the front stall received all the cash, he was not supposed to know the total. He just dropped every paisa he received into a long-necked bronze jug and brought it in at six o'clock, returned to his seat, and brought in another instalment in a smaller container at seven, when the shutters were drawn. Jagan would not count the cash yet but continued to read the Lord's sayings. Without looking up he was aware that the frying had stopped; he noticed the hissing of the oven when the fire died out, the clinking of pans and ladles being washed, and then the footsteps approaching him, four pairs of feet from the kitchen, and one pair from the front stall as trays of leftovers were brought in as the last act for the day. Then when he knew that all of them were assembled at his desk, he addressed in a general way a routine question, "How much is left over?"

"Not much."

"Be exact."

"Two seers of Mysore Pak."

"That we can sell tomorrow."

"Jilebi half a seer."

"Won't be so good tomorrow. All right, go."

The front-stall boy carried in the leftover trays and unobtrusively made his exit. The cooks still awaited his permission to leave. Jagan asked, "Are all the windows shut?"

"Yes."

Jagan now addressed himself to the head cook. "Tomorrow no jilebi? What is wrong with it?" It bothered him to think of the leftovers. They rankled in his mind as if he had a splinter under his skull. He loved to see clean shining trays return to the kitchen at the end of a day. A babble of argument followed. Jagan asked, "What do we do with the leftovers?"

The head cook said soothingly as usual, "We will try a new sweet tomorrow, if you will let me do it. There will be no problem of leftovers. We can always pulp everything back and fry them afresh in a new shape."

Jagan said philosophically, "After all, everything consists of flour, sugar, and flavours. . . ."—trying to come to a decision which he had been resisting all along; after all, one had to take a practical view, with the price of foodstuff going up.

When his staff was gone he put away his scripture book and pulled out his table drawer, which was padded with a folded towel in order to muffle the sound of coin being emptied from the bronze jug. His fingers quickly sorted out the denominations, the fives, tens, and quarters, with the flourish of a virtuoso running his fingers over a keyboard; his eyes swept the collection at a glance and arrived at the final count within fifteen minutes. He made an entry in a small notebook, and then more elaborate entries in a ledger which could be inspected by anyone. In his small notebook he entered only the cash that came in after six o'clock, out of the smaller jug. This cash was in an independent category; he viewed it as free cash, whatever that might mean, a sort of immaculate conception, self-generated, arising out of itself and entitled to survive without reference to any tax. It was converted into crisp currency at the earliest moment, tied into a bundle, and put away to keep company with the portrait of Mr. Noble in the loft at home.

Jagan gave a final look at the cash in the drawer, locked it carefully, tugged the handle four times, and pushed his chair back with a lot of noise. He put a huge brass lock on the door, turned the key and put it in his pocket, and said, "Captain! See if the lock is all right." The captain seized the lock in a martial grip as if it were a hand-grenade and gave it a final jerk. "This is a very strong lock, sir, can't get it nowadays. I know about locks; this must have been made in a village foundry." He expatiated on the world of locks and locksmiths. Jagan cut him short with, "Well, be watchful." The captain gave him a military salute, and that was the end of the day.

Chapter Two

A lull had fallen on Market Road when he walked back home at a little past seven-thirty. An enormous shaft of blue light fell on the road from the Krishna Dispensary. He noticed Dr. Krishna at his table peering at the throat of a patient. A street dog lay snoring on a heap of stone on the roadside, kept there since the first municipal body was elected in Free India in 1947 and meant for paving the road. A light was still seen under the door of Truth Printing although it was shut in deference to the Shopping Hours Act. Jagan knew that if he knocked Nataraj would open the door, and he could always have the excuse of asking if the book was ready. The book had been in the press for years out of count, his *magnum opus* on Nature Cure and Natural Diet. Jagan knew that Nataraj would say again that he was waiting for types, but he could always sit down in one of his chairs and discuss politics. He overcame the temptation and passed on. "Must be home, the boy will be lonely. Not today." He fell into a brooding and introspective state as he walked on the edge of the road and was alone with himself. Jutkas drove past him, the drivers urging their horses with shrill cries, and then a few cycles, a scooter, and a couple of cars loudly honking their horns.

The traffic thinned and disappeared and he knew that he had come past Kabir Lane, as no more light fell in the street from the shops. At the junction of Market Road and Lawley Extension there was a short parapet over a culvert. As usual the vagrant was sitting on it staring at passers-by and spitting into the gutter, and the donkey stood beside the wall as if it were offering itself for target practice. Jagan knew what the vagrant was waiting for: for the dining leaves to be cast out of the homes in Kabir Lane: he would collect them, scour them with his hands, and fill his belly with any vegetables and rice that might be left on them. "The remedy would be for our nation to change its habits, for people to eat off plates and not use leaves for the purpose: the plates could be washed and kept—unlike the leaves, which are thrown out after dinner for vagrants to pick," Jagan reflected. He was for a moment racked with the problem of national improvement in various directions. "If everyone gave up dining leaves, those engaged in the leaf trade would be thrown out of their profession and an alternative engagement would have to be found for them. But first statistics should be taken of the percentage of the population eating off leaves (and those eating off plates, what kind of plate? Silver, aluminium, or what metal?). How many were engaged in gathering the dry leaves from the forests of Mempi and stitching them with little splinters, and how many in cultivating special banana leaves used for dining? Till all this was done on a national scale this vagrant would continue to remain here." Late in the night he emerged from this culvert and went down the streets crying at every door, "Oh good mother, give a handful of rice for this hungry one. . . ." He had a deep voice which penetrated the door and reached the kitchen beyond; his tone also quietened troublesome children as he was described to be a man with three eyes. "He is a disgrace to the nation," Jagan commented within himself, and by the time he reached the statue of Lawley, a furlong off, his head throbbed with several national and human problems and their ramifications. Sir Frederick Lawley faced the city, and his back was supposed to be the back of beyond at one time, the limit of the city's expansion; but this prophecy was confounded when Lawley Extension, South Extension, and the New Extension all stretched out beyond the statue, and Jagan's ancestral home, which had been the last house outskirting the city, became the first one for all the newer colonies.

As Jagan approached the statue he felt a thrill, not at the spectacle of the enormous gentleman, standing in a Napoleonic attitude, benignly surveying the history and fortunes of Malgudi in a grand sweep (Jagan had ceased to notice the statue for over forty years now), but because he anticipated a glimpse of his son Mali on the other side of the statue. The pedestal had broad steps all around, which served as a park bench for the young and the old of the neighbourhood. Pensioners, idlers, tired workmen, sickly citizens advised by their doctors to inhale fresh air, sat facing east, west, north, and south on the steps. Students leaning on their cycles formed a group on the southern steps, all dressed in tight trousers and colourful shirts, hotly discussing film stars and cricket and fashions in dress and deportment. Jagan passed the statue on its north side so that he might not embarrass his son, but he liked to make sure that he was there; with a swift glance at the group, he spotted Mali by the deep yellow of his shirt, and the brief glimpse filled him with joy. He tiptoed away looking elsewhere, muttering to himself irrelevantly, "Poor boy, poor boy, let him be." He was very proud of his son's height, weight, and growth. "There are others, but he stands out from among them. Wonder what

God has in store for him," he reflected; "must give him more time." He reached home, his thoughts still hovering about his son.

He let himself into his house, switched on the light in the front room, took off his upper cloth and hung it on a nail in the wall, took off his jibba and thrust it into a basket for tomorrow's wash. He passed through the ancient house, through its triple series of open courtyards and corridors, and reached the back door, lifted the cross bar, and let it down gently. He stood for a moment gazing at the stars, enthralled at the spectacle of the firmament. "One still wonders," he told himself, "but the problem remains. Who lives in those? We are probably glimpsing the real Heaven and don't know it. Probably all our ancient sages are looking down at us. What are those constellations?" He couldn't be clear about them. His astronomy was limited to the location of the Pole Star from Orion's Belt or Sword or some such point, for which knowledge he had been awarded a second-class badge many years ago when he was a Boy Scout. For all the million stellar bodies sparkling, as far as Jagan was concerned, they might not be more than the two he had been taught to identify. In addition to Orion and the Pole Star he often noticed an extraordinarily lively firework in the sky, which sometimes stood poised over the earth in the westerly direction. He called it sometimes Venus, sometimes Jupiter, never being sure, but admiring it unreservedly and feeling proud that he was also a part of the same creation. All this was a habitual second of contemplation whenever he passed into the bathroom in the back yard.

The bathroom was a shack, roofed with corrugated sheets; beaten-out tin was fixed anyhow to a wooden frame to serve as a door on rusty hinges; the wooden frame was warped and the door never shut flush but always left a gap through which one obtained a partial glimpse of anyone bathing. But it had been a house practice, for generations, for its members not to look through. This bathroom remained very much what it had been in the days of his father, who had resisted all suggestions for improvement. "After all," he declared, "no one is expected to live in a bathroom; one had better come out of it soon so that the rest may have a chance of tidying themselves." A very tall coconut tree loomed over the bath, shedding enormous withered fronds and other horticultural odds and ends on the corrugated roof with a resounding thud. Everything in this home had the sanctity of usage, which was the reason why no improvement was possible. Jagan's father, as everyone knew, had lived at first in a thatched hut at the very back of this ground. Jagan remembered playing in a sand heap outside the hut; the floor of the hut was paved with cool clay, and one could put one's cheek to it on a warm day and feel heavenly. His father had also trained up a beanstalk onto the thatch and watched its development with anxiety. When he found some money, he put up the walls of the bathroom, laying the bricks with his own hands, and that became practically the starting point of the house. They fetched water from a well across the road and stored it in old kerosene tins and drums. His father expanded the house from the back yard to the front. As a child, Jagan had no notion how his father's fortune improved—although he heard vague words such as "appeal," "lawyers," "lower court," and "upper court." By the time he became an adult, capable of understanding these affairs, they were over and he never could explain what the litigations were about and against whom. There came a time when the hut was finally pulled down; its thatches were used for heating a cauldron of water for a bath, and the cool mud floor was torn up and dug into pits for planting coconut seedlings. His father spent a whole week in these operations. Jagan and his brothers carried off baskets of shovelled earth, screaming with delight, "Let us build a mountain." Father had his theories of coconut-rearing and filled the pits with great quantities of salt. "Salt is the only thing that can make a coconut tree grow," he remarked every day. "Show me the man who can grow a coconut tree properly and I will show you one with a practical head on his shoulders."

Regularly at five in the morning Jagan got up from bed, broke a twig from a margosa tree in the back yard, chewed its tip, and brushed his teeth. He was opposed to the use of a toothbrush. "The bristles are made of the hair from the pig's tail," he declared. "It's unthinkable that anyone should bite a pig's tail first thing in the morning." It was impossible to disentangle the sources of his theories and say what he owed to Mahatmaji and how much he had imbibed from his father, who had also spent a lifetime perfecting his theories of sound living and trying them on himself, his coconut trees, children, and wife. Even after the advent of nylon bristles Jagan never changed his views, maintaining that nylon had an adverse effect on the enamel. "You disbelieve me. Remember my father who died at ninety without a single tooth loose in his jaw." Jagan had immense faith in the properties of margosa, and in spite of its bitterness, he called it "Amrita," the ambrosia which kept the Gods alive; and sometimes he called it "Sanjeevini," the rare herb mentioned in the epics which, held at the nostrils, could bring the dead to life. He never ceased to feel grateful to his father for planting a seedling in his time and providing him with a perennial source of twigs—enough for his generation and the next, considering the dimensions of the tree. He chewed its bitter leaves once a month, as it destroyed all bacteria in the system, and he felt elated when the breeze blew—the air passing through the margosa boughs became an antityphoid agent, and during the summer rains the place became fragrant as the little yellow flowers drifted down like floss. He collected them, fried them in ghee, and consumed the ambrosia for all his worth once a week. His wife refused to associate herself with any of his health-giving activities. She hated his theories and lived her own life. Their first clash occurred when he forbade her to swallow aspirin and suggested that she should fry a little margosa flower in ghee and swallow it for relief from headache. Seated beside the ancient pillar in their courtyard, she had knotted a towel around her temples and swayed madly back and forth, desperately begging for aspirin. Jagan was very sympathetic, no doubt, but was convinced that aspirin would do her no good. She had just looked up at him and said, "Oh, this headache is not half as unbearable as your talk. You would sooner see me dead, I suppose."

"Your headache has made you crazy," he said, his temper rising. He hated her appearance with that silly towel knotted around her head and her dishevelled hair. She looked ghoulish and no wonder she suffered inexplicable headaches! He suddenly realized the trend of his thinking and suppressed it with a deliberate effort. "You may do what you like. Only don't suffer."

"Leave me alone," she had said in reply.

Jagan wanted to ask, "Why are you disgusted with me?" but passed on into Mali's room. Mali had insisted upon having a room of his own, and in that vast house it was not difficult to find him one. Mali got a long hall without a ventilator or window, known as the "cool room" in those days, which had a stone-topped round table at the centre and a stool, and Mali seemed delighted to be assigned this room, as it was near the kitchen and the main hall and he could enjoy privacy without losing sight of all the goings on in the house—such as the arguments between his father and mother or their conversation with visitors. He had a

I 7

few books heaped on the round table and some house-build-
ing blocks. Jagan had asked him, "Boy, do you know where
your mother keeps her headache pill?"

"I know, but she will not let me touch it."

"Why?"

"Because I may eat it. That's all. It looks so nice."

Jagan was scared. "Boy, don't you go near it; it is poison."

"What's poison?" asked the boy innocently, looking up
from a paper kite he was fiddling with.

"Oh," Jagan said rather desperately. He tried to avoid uttering inauspicious words but there seemed to be no other
way. He said, "People die when they eat poison."

Mali listened with interest and asked, "And then what?"
as if listening to a story. Matters seemed to be proceeding in
an unexpected direction. "Where is the pill?" Jagan asked.
The boy indicated the cupboard in the hall and cried, "On
the very top, so high that you all think I cannot reach it."
Jagan found his son's attraction to aspirin ominous. He
merely replied, "I'll get you better things to eat than this
pill. Forget it, you understand?"

Then he had gone to the cupboard and found the pill for
his wife. But that was some years ago, and Mali had grown.

Chapter Three

Mali said one morning, "I have an idea." Jagan felt slightly nervous and asked, "What may it be?" The boy paused while swallowing his breakfast. "I can't study any more."

The father was aghast. "Anyone been rude to you in the college?"

"Let them try!" said the boy.

"Tell me what's happened."

"Nothing," said the boy. "I do not find it interesting, that's all," and he went on munching his food with his eyes down. Jagan had never seen him so serious. The boy seemed to have suddenly grown up. He had never spoken to his father in this tone before.

Jagan merely repeated, "If it's something I can do, tell me."

"I don't want to study, that's all," repeated the boy.

The morning sun came through a glass tile and touched up with radiance the little heap of uppumav on his plate—a piece of green chili and some globules of oil made the stuff sparkle, catching Jagan's eye insistently for a moment, making him wonder if he had made some strange edible gem-set for his son rather than merely frying semolina and spicing it. Shaking himself out of this fantasy, he said, "All right, I'll come to your college and speak to those people."

The boy looked up angrily. In his anxiety to communicate a new idea to his father, he had become brusque and aggressive. His face was flushed.

"So early in the morning, and the boy showing such a temper!" Jagan reflected, as if temper had an approved timetable. "All right, get on with your eating. We'll talk of these things later," he mumbled, when he should have said, "Swallow your food and run off to your class." He was a cowardly father and felt afraid to mention class or college. The boy might scream at the mention of the college or kick away his breakfast. Jagan had an almost maternal obsession about the boy's feeding. At home he spent all his time cooking for his son; it had started when his wife had her first attack of brain fever and was taken to the hospital. When he was old enough to notice things, Mali had asked, "Father, why don't you engage a cook?"

"I don't believe in engaging any cook."

"Why not?"

"Do we engage a servant to do the breathing for us? Food is similar."

"Oh, Father! Father!" the boy cried, "Don't you engage cooks in your sweetmeat shop?"

"Oh, that's different. It's like a factory and they are specialists and technicians," said Jagan, giving full rein to his imagination.

The boy failed to grasp the distinction and cried desperately, "I do not want you to cook for me hereafter. We have our college canteen. I can look after myself." He had stuck to it, relaxing his resolution only to the extent of accepting the breakfast made by Jagan. The practice had continued. Particularly after his wife's death, Jagan became obsessed with his son's diet and brooded over the question night and day. At night before retiring, he held a long conference with his son on not only what he had eaten during the day but what he would prefer to eat next day. The son, cornered at this hour, answered in his usual manner of half-syllables and clipped sentences, and the day would conclude with Jagan's exposition of his usual theories of nutrition, halfway through which Mali would turn away and bolt the door of his room, leaving Jagan with his unfinished sentence. He would spend a few moments staring at the door, then rise and unroll his mat in the open veranda in the second block and fall asleep before the gong at the Taluk Office sounded nine.

Now he felt desperate to know what his son would do if he left the college—or rather the college canteen. He asked idiotically, "Where will you eat?"

His son smiled grimly and replied, "Why do you bother when you keep saying one need not eat?" He put on his yellow shirt, picked up his bicycle, and was off.

Jagan had to bottle up his confusions until the arrival of his cousin in the evening. "Come here," he cried the moment he sighted him—much to the bewilderment of the cousin, who wanted first of all to go through and try the sweets as they came out of the frying pan. He flourished his arms as if to say, "Your banalities can wait," and passed on. Jagan saw him disappear into the kitchen with resignation. "He is bound to come out sooner or later. No one can stay long in all that heat and smoke. Moreover, he will reach satiety soon with those sweets. . . ."

Market Road suddenly became alive with the shouts of school children just let off. A few of them, satchels slung on their shoulders, as usual stood in front of the Sweet Mart gaping at the display beyond the glass. Jagan watched them from his seat without emotion. "It's up to their parents to provide them with the money for sweets. I can't be handing out charity packets." He felt apologetic sitting there and collecting the cash—a vestige of conscience from his day of public service. If the public could have joined and sub- scribed, he'd have given away a portion of his profits in order to provide sweets for every child that gazed at his counter. "But this is a poor country, sir. Per capita income is three annas." He still stuck to the figure that he had got out of a book called *Poverty and Un-British Rule in India,* in his college days. But this figure restrained him from demanding of every parent in the town that he spend eight annas a day at his shop. "Poor country! Most people cannot afford even rice for two meals a day. When I cease to be a merchant, I'll— But sugar costs one and thirty per kilogram and flour and butter, real or fake, cost thrice as much and what about the seasoning? Nutmegs, seventy paise each—mark it, each! They used to be got in handfuls for the smallest coin; and what halva would be worth its name if you did not crush a little nutmeg into it?"

When the cousin emerged from the kitchen wiping his mouth with the towel, Jagan said, as a continuation of his thoughts on social problems, which for the moment swamped his private sorrows, "Do you realize how few ever really understand how fortunate they are in their circumstances?"

The cousin nodded a general approval, secretly puzzled as to what this profound thinker might be driving at. "They all forget or get used to things; that's the way of the world," he said, smacking his lips and stating a philosophy that could fit any circumstance.

"Especially young men," said Jagan, "they are a problem everywhere. I was reading a little while ago somewhere"— and tried to quote from some sort of report on the youth of today, although he could not remember where he had read it or what it said.

"It takes one nowhere," said the cousin, sympathetically, his mind gloating over the memory of the sweets he had eaten.

The conversation was proceeding smoothly thus, when Jagan said abruptly, "Mali is displaying strange notions."

The cousin opened his eyes widely to register the appropriate reaction, not being certain how critical he could sound of Mali. Jagan explained. The cousin suddenly assumed a definite stand and said, "It'd be best to know what the boy is thinking, our educational methods being what they are today." You could always hit education if you had no other target.

"I was always hoping that he'd be a graduate and that's the basic qualification one should have, don't you think so?" Jagan added with a sigh, "If I had passed the B.A., I could have done so many other things."

"But it was not to be, and yet what's lacking in your present state?"

"I had to leave the college when Gandhi ordered us to non-cooperate. I spent the best of my student years in prison," said Jagan, feeling heroic, his reminiscent mood slurring over the fact that he had failed several times in the B.A., had ceased to attend the college, and had begun to take his examinations as a private candidate, long before the call of Gandhi. "But what excuse can these boys have for refusing to study?" he asked.

The cousin, ever a man of caution, repeated, "It's worth finding out from the boy himself. Why didn't you have a talk with him?"

"Why don't you?" asked Jagan in a tone of pointless challenge, and added sentimentally, "He has called you 'uncle' ever since he could lisp the syllable."

"The only person to whom I'm not a cousin," said the gentleman, and both of them laughed.

The serious burden of life returning to Jagan presently, he said, "You must do something about it and tell me to-night."

At ten that night, the cousin came up and knocked on the door softly. Jagan, for once, was awake after nine. The boy had retired and shut himself in his room without giving his father a chance to refer to the day's events. Jagan had noticed the light burning in his room and resisted an impulse to peep through the keyhole. "I wish you had peeped in—you'd have seen what he was doing," said the cousin, when they had stolen on tiptoe from Jagan's house, strolled down the road to the foot of the Lawley Statue, and settled comfortably on the granite platform there. The cool night air was blowing on their faces. Sir Frederick loomed over them aggressively with his head amidst the stars.

"What do you mean?" said Jagan, leaning back in the shadow of Sir Frederick's spurs. All kinds of morbid and terrifying speculations arose in Jagan's mind. Was the boy counterfeiting money or murdering someone? A hundred evil possibilities occurred to him. He gripped the other's wrist and commanded, "Tell me everything without concealing anything."

The cousin shook off the hold contemptuously. "He is writing, that's all. Wants to be a writer."

"Writer" meant in Jagan's dictionary only one thing—a "clerk"—an Anglo-Indian, colonial term since the days when Macaulay had devised a system of education to provide a constant supply of clerical staff for the East India Company. Jagan felt aghast. Here he was trying to shape the boy into an aristocrat with a bicycle, college life, striped shirts, and everything, and he wanted to be a "writer"! Strange!

"Why does he want to be a writer?" he asked.

"I don't know. You will have to ask him."

"Where does he want to work? It's degrading!" he cried, "after all the trouble I have taken to build up a reputation and a status!" He beat his brow in despair.

It never occurred to the cousin that Jagan had misunderstood the word "writer." He said, "I lost no time after you had told me this evening to go out in search of the boy. I waited at the college gate—"

"Oh, did he go to his college after all?" cried Jagan ecstatically, concluding that he must have eaten in the canteen.

"Yes," replied the cousin. "It was only a farewell visit. I saw him come out with a gang of friends, who patted his back and shook his hand and did all sorts of things. A couple of teachers came out, looked at him, and said something. I heard him say, 'My father has other plans—probably he is sending me to America.'"

"Ah!" Jagan exclaimed. "What'll he do in America? America indeed!"

"Don't be hasty," said the cousin slowly. "He had to tell them something before leaving the college. Until he demands to be sent to America, don't take notice of it."

"All sorts of ideas! All sorts of ideas!" Jagan cried helplessly, tapping his fingers on the granite.

"Well, he may become a second Bharati or Tagore or Shakespeare some day. How can you judge now?" the cousin said.

The truth finally dawned on Jagan. "Oh, how stupid am I? Yes, of course, 'writer,' I know. I've become illiterate, I think," he cried happily. It was a great relief that the son was not attempting to be the other kind of writer.

"What else did you think?" the cousin asked, and added, "I have heard that writers earn a lot of money nowadays. They become famous."

"What does he want to write?"

"I don't know. Poetry, perhaps, easiest to start with, or stories. What else do people write?" said the cousin, not wanting to flounder in unknown seas. "Actually, it was difficult to get even that out of him. I met him at his school—"

"College," corrected Jagan, feeling somewhat piqued.

"Yes, yes, I meant college. I always think of Mali as a little fellow, and it's very difficult to remember that he is no longer a mere schoolboy. At his college gate, when the teachers left him, he saw me and stopped to ask what had brought me there. I didn't want to seem officious, and so said something or other and then asked if he would come for a cup of coffee somewhere. 'Not just coffee,' he said, 'I want a lot to eat as well.'"

"Poor boy, he must have been starving," cried Jagan, feeling anguished.

"Not necessarily," said the cousin. "Young men eat and still wish to eat a lot more, you know."

"Certainly," cried Jagan. "What is there to prevent his eating as much as he likes and at all hours of the day?"

"Do you leave enough cash with him?"

"Of course I do," said Jagan. "Did he say anything about it?"

"Oh, no, oh, no," cried the cousin. "He is not that sort of young man. Even if you starved him and denied him everything he'd never complain."

Jagan felt proud at the encomiums heaped on his son. He remained thoughtful, while the stars in the sky paused in their course. A couple of dogs trotted in a chase. The vagrant stirred in his sleep, muttering to himself on the other side of the statue. Jagan peeped around and said, "Disgraceful that our nation cannot attack this problem of vagrants. Must do something about it, when I find the time."

The cousin ignored this larger social problem and continued, "I took him to the Ananda Bhavan; you know that place is noisy, the loud-speaker deafening you all the time."

Jagan implored, "I want to hear nothing about the Ananda Bhavan Restaurant. Tell me about the boy, please."

"Yes, yes, be patient. I know you don't like the Ananda Bhavan people. I know they tried to blackmail you with the sales tax."

"Oh, please stick to the point. I don't care what they do or did. Tell me what the boy said. Was he unhappy?"

"Yes and no. Happy that he was going to be free to be a writer, unhappy that you should expect him to study at—"

"The college," completed Jagan, almost afraid lest the man should blunder into saying "school" again.

The cousin took the hint and said, "College, college, and of course college. The very word drives him crazy, although you like it so much. He hates his lessons; he hates his syllabus and all his books. The very thought infuriates him. Do you know what he did? He had his class-books in his hand. I had ordered dosais for him and we were waiting. He suddenly tore up the pages of his books savagely, beckoned an attendant, and said, 'Put these in the fire in the kitchen.' "

"Could you not stop him? Didn't you tell him that books must be treated respectfully, being a form of the goddess Saraswathi? How could this boy ever pass his B.A.?"

"I don't know," said the cousin reflectively. "It didn't occur to me to argue with him, that's all; what use would it be anyway?"

"Are you also mad?" cried Jagan. "Don't you see . . ."

The cousin said, "No. When he tore the books it seemed very appropriate, our education being what it is. . . ."

"Oh, stop it. I hope you have not been telling him things."

The cousin ignored this insinuation and said, "Do you know what he said after sending his books to the fire? He made up a verse on the spot: 'Let us show gratitude to the Great Fire that consumes our horrid books—' or something like it. It sounded very smart and sensible. He ate dosais and a number of things, the total bill being three rupees."

"Great boy," said Jagan, gratified by his son's verse as well as his gluttony. "I'll reimburse you. Remind me at the shop tomorrow."

"No hurry, no hurry. You can take your own time to return it to me," said the cousin.

It seemed difficult to keep to the point, there being no precise point to keep to, no main subject to return to. They went on rambling thus until the Taluk Office gong sounded twelve o'clock. It boomed through the silent town, and Jagan said, "Even burglars will have gone home to sleep, but still I have got nowhere. I don't know why he cannot write and also read his college books."

"He said that the one interfered with the other," explained the cousin.

After a brief pause, Jagan suddenly asked, "Was Shakespeare a B.A.?"—a question that no one could answer in that place.

The cousin said, "Why go so far? I know Kalidasa never went to a college."

"Because there were no colleges three thousand years ago," said Jagan.

"How can you know whether there were colleges or not?" asked the cousin.

"College or no college, I know Kalidasa was a village idiot and a shepherd until the goddess Saraswathi made a scratch on his tongue and then he burst into that song, *Syamala-dandakam*, and wrote his *Sakuntala*. I know the story. I have heard it often enough," said Jagan.

"If you know the story, you must believe in it and hope that some day Mali will be another Kalidasa," said the cousin soothingly.

Jagan, at the earliest opportunity, applied his eye to the keyhole of Mali's door, which remained shut most hours of the day. The boy seemed to be avoiding him. Jagan prepared the breakfast and left it on the hall table, and also tucked a five-rupee note under the plate so that the boy might eat wherever he liked the rest of the day. Mali went out and returned home at some hour of the night and shut himself in. Jagan went about his sweet-making without any outward sign of agitation, but inside he was all torn up. He could not understand where his son spent the day, or what he ate. He had never suspected that his zeal for education was going to ruin their relationship. He wanted to make it up with his son.

Through the keyhole he saw the light burning in Mali's room. He saw Mali sitting on a stool with his elbow on the table, just brooding. He felt disappointed that the boy was not writing. He had imagined the writer burning the midnight oil and littering the table with sheets of paper in a delirium of inspiration: Kalidasa suddenly bursting into inspired song, the walls of the ancient house reverberating with a new song to be on everybody's lips for a thousand years to come. But the picture that presented itself to him now was different. The boy seemed to be moping in dejection and boredom. It was time to pull him out of it. Jagan realized that the time had come for him to forget college education and get completely identified with Mali's fantasies, at least until he came out of his gloom. He beat upon the door with both fists, stooping and squinting at the keyhole having proved irksome.

"What's happened? Why are you bringing down the house?" asked the boy, opening the door.

Jagan pushed his way in announcing, "Boy, I like your

idea. Come on, let us talk about it." He breezily paced around and sat on a stool. The boy followed him mutely, his misgivings not totally gone. Jagan smoothed his own brow and the corners of his face so that there should be not the slightest trace of a frown and managed to give his face an affable grin, exuding an impression of total approval. They stared at each other uncomfortably for a second, and then the son came over and sat on the circular table with a marble top.

Jagan asked soothingly, "Do you want a good table?"

"What for?" asked the boy, poised between doubt and trust. The slightest pressure at the wrong place could topple him over to the wrong side. And so Jagan said, "A writer needs a lot of space for his manuscripts—they are precious, you know." The boy was evidently pleased that the new table was not being planned for bearing college books and notes.

"Who has told you about me?"

"These things become known. A writer has to come out!" He was amazed at his own fluency.

"I don't care either way!"

Jagan looked about. There was no sign of a book in the making. The marble top was clean, all the college books having been swept out of view. He felt a moment's curiosity about their fate, but checked himself. Not his business, anyway.

"Do you want me to buy you white paper? Have you got a good pen? I think I had better get you a new desk with a lot of drawers." Peace and understanding were returning after all, and they could grope their way through the world of letters now, each thinking that the other might know better. "What are you writing now?" asked Jagan with the humility of a junior reporter interviewing a celebrity.

"A novel," the boy said condescendingly.

"Oh, wonderful. Where did you learn to write novels?" Mali did not answer the question. Jagan repeated it.

"Are you examining me?" Mali asked.

"Oh, no, I'm just interested, that's all. What story are you writing?"

"I can't tell you now. It may turn out to be a poem after all. I don't know."

"But don't you know what you are going to write when you sit down to write?"

"No," said the boy haughtily. "It's not like frying sweets in your shop."

This was completely mystifying to the junior reporter. He said pathetically, "Tell me if you want my help in any matter."

The boy received that in sullen silence.

"Are your friends also writers?"

"How can they be? They are only readers and want to get their degrees. That's all." Jagan rigorously suppressed his approval of those friends' attitude. The boy added, "They are all ordinary fellows who are not good for anything else."

"I thought you were fond of your friends," Jagan said, seizing every opportunity to acquire a better understanding of his son's mind. He had thought that the friends were dear to the boy, the way they stood beside the statue leaning on their bicycles and talking loudly. It was also a slight matter of relief, for Jagan had had a fear that his friends might be misleading the boy; now it was some satisfaction to know that he was going astray entirely through his own individual effort. "For twenty years," Jagan reflected, "he has grown up with me, under the same roof, but how little I have known him! But the boy has been up to something. He will count for something sooner or later."

"I saw in *Ananda Vikatan* a competition for novels," Mali explained. "They will pay twenty-five thousand rupees for the best."

"On what conditions?"

"It must be sent before September thirtieth, that's all, and a coupon in the magazine must be filled in."

Jagan leaned over to study the dates on a calendar on the wall. "This is just May."

"I know," snapped the boy. "I've five months."

"Have you begun to write?" Jagan asked timidly.

"I am not the sort to show my story to anyone before I finish it."

"What's the story?" asked Jagan, persisting.

The boy shrank away from him and repeated, "Are you examining me?" in an ominous manner.

"Oh, no, it's not that."

"You don't believe me, I know," said the boy half despairingly.

Jagan was for a moment confused. He reaffirmed his faith in his son in the loudest terms possible. Secretly his mind was bothered as to why there was always an invisible barrier between them. He had never been harsh to the boy; so long as he could remember, he had always got him whatever he wanted these twenty-odd years; during the last ten particularly he had become excessively considerate, after the boy lost his mother.

The scene remained forever fresh in Jagan's memory—that terrible Friday when their doctor, Krishna, had observed her breathing and said, "No doctor could do more, a very rare type of brain tumour, if one knew why it came, one would also know how to get rid of it." It was nearing midnight and the doctor had been in continuous attendance for forty-eight hours with needle, oxygen, and ice-bag, sparing no apparatus in order to save a life: he was physically worn out in the effort and driven nearly mad by Jagan's hints that Nature Cure might have benefited her. "Nature!" he snapped irritably, turning his head from the bed. "Nature would sooner see us dead. She has no use for a brain affected by malignant growth, that's all. . . ."

Jagan had shut his mouth, feeling that the moment was inappropriate for his theories. But when the doctor took his final leave and moved off to his car, Jagan, following him out, could not help putting in a word on the subject. "You'll see for yourself, Doctor, when I publish my book. I've all the material for it."

The doctor made an impatient gesture, and said, "Go back, go back to your wife for the few hours left. Your son is watching us. Protect him."

Turning back from the car, Jagan saw Mali at the door with bewilderment in his eyes. It was harrowing to look at his thin, scraggy frame (he developed and grew tall and broad suddenly after his eighteenth birthday). The boy asked, "What did the doctor say?" He had been attending on his mother for many weeks now. In her rare moments of lucidity she beckoned to him, and accepted the diet if he fed her. He came running home from school in order to feed her, rarely going out to play with his friends. At the boy's question, Jagan lost his nerve completely, held his son's hands, and broke into a loud wail. Mali had shaken himself off and watched his father from a distance with a look of dismay and puzzlement.

Even with the passage of time, Jagan never got over the memory of that moment. The coarse, raw pain he had felt at the sight of Mali on that fateful day remained petrified in some vital centre of his being. From that day, the barrier had come into being. The boy had ceased to speak to him normally.

"Oh, no!" apologized Jagan, "I'm sure you are going to

write something good, my boy. I do not in the least doubt it. I just wanted to know the story, that's all. You know how much I like stories. Do you remember the stories I used to tell you at night? The one about a black monkey which you used to like so much!" After taking complete charge of his son, he used to divert his mind by telling him stories from the Panchatantra. The boy showed no sign that he remembered those days or wanted to be reminded of them. He showed no reaction. Jagan said, "You know I'm also a kind of writer. You will know more about it when Truth Printing lets it out of the press." And he laughed in a hollow manner.

The boy said simply, "Father, you do not understand. I want to write something different."

"Of course, of course . . . Tell me if you need my help."

It seemed a very simple way of earning twenty-five thousand rupees without frying or baking anything. They sat talking until one in the morning, while Jagan was subjected to a revelation every other minute. He learnt that the boy had cut out the coupon from the magazine on his college library table, risking punishment and humiliation if caught. "I did it with a blade, under the very nose of the librarian," the boy said with a hint of laughter.

"Would that be the right thing to do?" Jagan asked, puzzled.

"Of course, how else could I get the coupon?" the boy asked, producing it from within the pages of a small pocket diary.

Jagan said, looking at it, "If this is from *Vikatan* you could have bought a copy for four annas, or as many copies as you needed."

"That anyone could do," the boy said, and added mysteriously, "I have always wanted to teach that librarian a lesson; he always thought he was too clever."

Jagan derived a peculiar thrill in speaking of his son as a writer. Next day, on the way to his Sweet Mart, he stopped at least three acquaintances on the road and spoke to them of his son. The fourth person to be told was the head cook. As soon as he arrived, Jagan summoned him to his throne and said, "My son is writing a book." The head cook, between thoughts of the frying for the day, said it was a grand piece of news and evinced interest in the literary progress of Mali.

"He is going to earn twenty-five thousand rupees out of it, and he says he is going to finish it before September, wonderful boy! I never knew that my son was such a genius. Actually, you know, he need not do all this to get twenty-five thousand; that's always there. But I don't want to give it to him to handle. It's not like my generation; we came under the spell of Gandhi and could do no wrong."

"For all your wealth, you are such a simple man, eating nothing."

"Eating to live, that's all," corrected Jagan. "You will know when my book is printed. I'm also a sort of writer, you understand?"

"No wonder your son takes to it so happily," said the cook.

The cousin came at the usual hour, and heard the story. Jagan repeated himself and concluded, "I hope he will also emulate my philosophy of living. Simple living and high thinking, as Gandhi has taught us."

"True, true. But what I don't understand is why you should run a trade, make money, and accumulate it."

"I do not accumulate, it just grows naturally," said Jagan.

"What can I do? Moreover, I work, because it's one's duty to work." He pulled the drawer, took out his Bhagavad Gita, and read from it. "You see, it's my duty to go on doing something. Moreover"—he raised his voice—"that man, and the other one, and the one here, it supports them. What would our head cook do if it weren't for this establishment?"

"He'd probably be frying stuff in some other kitchen. He is a master fryer who'll get a job anywhere."

"It's not that, my dear fellow. Mine is the biggest sweetshop in the country. Have you any doubt about it?"

"None whatever; and your fry-master makes unadulterated good stuff."

Jagan felt soothed by this flattery. All the same he said, "No wonder Mali wants to try a new line. There are bound to be changes of outlook from generation to generation. Otherwise there will be no progress," he added in a sudden outburst of theorizing, once again a vestige of his Satyagraha days. It was as agreeable as the fragrance of the ghee, nutmeg, and saffron which emanated from the kitchen. He suddenly said, without any provocation, "I have always resisted the use of essences for flavouring or colouring. You can get any flavour from Germany; it is easy to deceive even the most fastidious nowadays."

"How false and illusory!" commented the cousin, in a philosophical strain.

"But I'll never use them as long as I am the master of this establishment," asserted Jagan. The cousin, as a sampler flourishing on absolute purity every afternoon, expressed unqualified approval of this statement.

Chapter Four

Peace reigned at home, with speech reduced to a minimum between father and son. Mali seemed to have brightened up at the fact that he wouldn't be expected to study. Jagan continued to feel gratified that his son was pursuing a fresh course, all his own. "Instead of reading other people's books, he is providing reading for others," he often reflected with a lot of pride. "He is doing a service in his own way." When he remembered the word "service," any activity became touched with significance. "Service" intoxicated him, sent a thrill through his whole being, and explained everything. The first time he heard the word was in 1937 when Mahatma Gandhi had visited Malgudi and addressed a vast gathering on the sands of the river. He spoke of "service," explaining how every human action acquired a meaning when it was performed as a service. Inspired by this definition, Jagan joined the movement for freeing India from foreign rule, gave up his studies, home, and normal life, and violated the British laws of the time. Neither the beatings from the police nor the successive periods of prison terms ever touched him when he remembered that he was performing a "service." "Everyone should be free to serve humanity in his own way," he told himself, and, "Mali is really helping mankind with his writing. What does he really write?" he often wondered. Stories? What sort of stories? Poems? Or did he write philosophy? He had a passing misgiving about his son's experience of life, his equipment to be a writer. He had uneasy thoughts sometimes when he sat on his throne in the shop looking at the pages of the Bhagavad Gita. However profound the lines before him might be, his own thoughts seemed to be stronger and capable of pushing aside all philosophy while revolving round the subject of Mali's manuscript. He wanted to know which language his Muses accepted, whether Tamil or English. If he wrote in Tamil he would be recognized at home; if in English, he would be known in other countries too. But did he know enough English, Tamil, or any language? He felt worried; his mind was racked with questions. The simplest solution of questioning Mali directly seemed impracticable. What could they discuss? Mali seemed to have become detached, more detached than ever. The only link between them was the five-rupee currency note that he left on the hall table every morning and checked later to find out if it had been accepted. Perhaps the boy lunched and dined at the Ananda Bhavan; it was galling to think that his money should find its way into the Ananda Bhavan cash desk. It could not be helped; it was supposed to be the best restaurant in the town; but Jagan knew that they did not use pure ghee but only hydrogenated vegetable oil in unlabelled tins—they were naïve enough to think that if the tins were unlabelled the public would take them to be real butter!

It was long past the thirtieth of September, and Jagan would have given anything to know if the manuscript had gone off. But there had been no sign of it anywhere. The boy's movements were so finely adjusted out of his own orbit that though they lived under one roof they might be in two different worlds. When he saw the light through the chink in the door, Jagan knew that the boy was in his room. He dared not knock on it. Rarely did they ever reach home at the same time, so there was no chance of their meeting in the hall. Jagan felt harrowed by the lack of information. When the cousin arrived at his appointed time, he found Jagan looking so restless that he felt constrained to remark as he emerged from the kitchen, "Every gift of life you are blessed with: what ninety out of a hundred people crave for—money; and what a hundred out of a hundred crave for—contentment. Yet you have not mastered one thing, that's the art of looking happy. You are always looking careworn."

"If one looks worn out by cares, God knows one must have sufficient cause. Do you see Mali at all?"

"Not much. No. No. Long ago, I saw him on a cycle one afternoon in Vinayak Street. Don't ask me what I was doing there. I generally go even farther than that when I have some work—always in the service of someone else, you may be sure. I do nothing for myself."

"Did he speak to you?"

"Of course not. He was riding a bicycle, I told you."

"What was he doing so far away?"

"Why not ask him?" asked the cousin.

"He won't answer, that's all," said Jagan.

"Have you tried?"

"No."

"Then try."

"He may resent the question and think I'm interfering."

"If I meet him, I'll find out, if you like."

"Please don't. He'll think I have set you on him."

"Of course, I'll tell him that I'm talking for you."

Jagan looked scared on hearing this. The cousin could

not help remarking, "You puzzle me. Why are you frightened?"

"I hate to upset him, that's all. I have never upset him in all my life."

"That means you have carried things to a point where you cannot speak to him at all."

"It's not that," said Jagan, not willing to accept this view.

"Can you tell me when you had your last conversation with him?"

There was a pause while Jagan threw his mind back. The cousin watched him ruthlessly, gently sucking the sweet on his tongue. Jagan remembered that their last speech had been three and a half months ago. He had been reading the paper in the hall, and his son had come out of his room.

"Ready to go out?"

"H'm."

That had terrified Jagan, and at once he had covered up any hint of inquisitiveness. "Did you see today's paper?"

"No."

"Don't you want to?"

"Nothing in it for me." The boy had walked across the hall.

Jagan could hear the cycle being taken off its spring stand, and the front door slamming. He sat still with his eyes glued to the newspaper. "God be thanked that there is no direct exit from his room to the street as my father once foolishly planned; otherwise I'd have lost the memory of my son's identity long ago."

Reporting this meeting to the cousin was just out of the question, so he said, "The trouble is our hours are so different. By the time I open my eyes from prayer, he's gone; it's been a time-honoured custom in our house not to disturb me when I am praying. But that's all beside the point. We are straying away from the subject. I want you to help me. Please find out, as if you were doing it on your own, where he goes every day, and what happened to the story. Did he finish it? Try to meet him and give me some information, please. I'll be grateful for your help."

"No, no; it's my duty to be of service to you. Don't thank me. I'll see what I can do in my humble way." He swelled with the importance of the undertaking. Jagan felt relieved.

The cousin came back four days later, took his seat beside the throne, and said, "New things are coming your way; your son wants to go to America. Didn't I hint to you long ago that it was coming?"

The first shock of the impact blanked out Jagan's mind for a time, and he caught his breath as he had a momentary panic at the thought of his son's removing himself geographically so far. He inanely repeated, "America! Why America? What has happened to his book? Has he written it? Hasn't he written it?"

"He thinks he will have to learn the art in America."

Jagan was furious at this notion; it was outrageous and hurt his national pride.

"Going there to learn storytelling! He should rather go to a village granny," he said, all his patriotic sentiments surging.

"Exactly what I told him," echoed the cousin.

"Did Valmiki go to America or Germany in order to learn to write his *Ramayana*?" asked Jagan with pugnacity. "Strange notions these boys get nowadays!" he said, avoiding gently any specific reference to his son.

The head cook interrupted at this point, bringing in the flavour of kitchen smoke, in order to announce, "Saffron stock out. Will last only another day." Jagan looked at him bemusedly, not able to grasp the subject clearly. The cousin answered for him and promised to arrange for a fresh supply. When the cook retreated into the kitchen, Jagan asked, "Have you found out where he spends his day?"

"At the Town Public Library."

"Where is it?" asked Jagan, never having dreamt that his town possessed a library. The cousin himself was not sure and flourished his arms vaguely in the direction of the river. "Must be one of those things for which a foundation stone is laid whenever a minister visits this town."

"I'd have known about it if it had been a thing of any importance. Anyway, do they let him live there?"

"He seems to like it, and does some amount of work there."

"What sort of work?" asked Jagan, appalled at the notion that Mali should have become a library assistant, of all things! "What has happened to his book?" he asked desperately.

"He will write it in America," said the cousin.

Jagan felt completely crushed; adverse forces seemed to hem him on all sides. "What has America to do with writing his book?"

"He has read in one of the magazines at the library about a college where they teach novel-writing."

Jagan once again felt like bursting out about Valmiki or a village granny, but restrained himself: "What happened to the prize?"

"Perhaps it's gone. He hasn't written the book yet," said the cousin. "Anyway, a book cannot be rushed."

"True, true," Jagan said, suddenly remembering his son's words the other night; but added as his own contribution to the theory of writing, "Still, I suppose, a book has to be written."

They spent a little time brooding over the mechanics of book production. "Why America?" asked Jagan, ignoring the instalment of cash that was brought in, while the cousin made no effort to leave.

"Because, perhaps, it's the only country where they teach such things."

"They eat only beef and pork in that country. I used to know a man from America, and he told me . . ."

"They also take a lot of intoxicating drinks, never water or milk," said the cousin, contributing his own bit of information. "And the women are free," he added. "I have seen some of their magazines about films; their women mix freely with men and snap off marriages without ado, and bask in the sun without clothes."

"Where did you see all this?" asked Jagan, and did not note the answer from the cousin, who flourished his arms vaguely. Jagan went on to say, "It may not all be true," not wishing to think a country to which Mali was going could be one to corrupt his body with wine, women, and meat, and his soul with other things. He said with a sudden determination, "But it's unthinkable. Mali shall stay here."

The cousin smiled cynically. Jagan had a momentary stab of suspicion that this man was at the back of it all. But the doubt passed.

The cousin said, "He has made all kinds of preparations."

"Without my permission or help!" cried Jagan.

"They have a typewriter at the library and he has been using it."

Partly filled with admiration, and partly enraged at the thought of the library, Jagan shouted suddenly, without thinking of what he was saying, "If they are going to make use of the library for such nefarious activities . . ."

The cousin said, "Did you know that he had gone to Madras for a few days?"

"No. Without my permission or help, without telling me

anything? I thought he was in his room." He remembered that the five-rupee notes left by him had not been picked up on certain days. Thinking that the boy had been saving, he had withheld the allowance, hoping to be asked.

"He has fixed his passport and other such things."

"How is he going to find the fare?"

"He says he has got it; he said he always knew where to find the money in the house."

Jagan felt shocked for a moment, but he also felt a sneaking admiration. "The boy is very practical," he said with feeling. He sat brooding for some time and then said, trying to put on a happy look, "See how self-reliant he has grown! I have always believed in leaving the entity to develop by itself, without relying on extraneous support. As they say in the Gita: 'Every soul is God. . . .' "

"And God can always look after himself," added the cousin.

"That's the whole point," said Jagan. "That's why I never wished to interfere when he suddenly decided to end his education. I said to myself, 'Perhaps he wants to educate himself in the school of life,' and left him free"—echoing various titbits of banality he had picked up in the course of his life and haphazard reading.

The cousin said, "Exactly my principle in life. I know so much about people and their problems and of the world. Did I go to a college to learn the art of living?"

"But I am surprised that he still thinks he can learn the art of writing from an American school!" He sniggered gently at the thought. "As my good cousin, please try and stop him. I don't know how I can live in that house without him. The very thought depresses me."

"Yes, I will," said the cousin mechanically, without conviction. "But do you know that he has worked out the details minutely? He is getting his American clothes made in Madras."

"I have always told him to buy a lot of clothes; especially in foreign countries one must always wear tie and shoes and such things, morning till night. Does he want any sort of help from me?" Jagan asked pathetically, almost appealing to the cousin to intercede and do something about it.

"What can you do?" asked the cousin brutally.

"I have a friend in Madras, a deputy minister, who was my prison-mate in those days in Bellary jail."

"No harm in trying your friend, but Mali needs no help from us. The librarian has a brother in the aeroplane company and he has done everything for Mali."

"Is he going to fly?" asked Jagan, panic-stricken.

"Who does not nowadays?"

Jagan almost wept as he said, "Please tell him to go by steamer. It's safer. Let him be safe. I don't like aeroplanes."

"He has almost paid for the air ticket," said the cousin, enjoying Jagan's predicament.

"It must be very costly," said Jagan, like a prattling baby.

"But he has doubtless found the cash for it," said the cousin.

"Naturally. What is the cash worth to me? It's all for him. He can have everything he wants," said Jagan, making a note mentally to count at the earliest moment his cash hoarded in the loft. He also considered transferring it all, in due course, to a casket behind the family Gods in the puja room.

At dead of night, he put up the ladder and climbed the loft. About ten thousand rupees had been extracted from the bundled currency. He calculated: "About four or five thousand rupees for passage; and the balance for clothes and other things. He should ask for more if he wants it, and of course, a monthly remittance later. Why should he not?" He heard the front door open; he put out the torch and sat still until he felt sure that Mali had safely locked himself in, feeling like a burglar himself, instead of one whose cash had been extracted.

Chapter Five

He had never thought that he could feel so superior about it. Now it seemed to him worth all the money and the pangs of separation. "My son is in America," he said to a dozen persons every day, puffing with pride on each occasion. It delayed his daily routine. On his way to the shop he had only to detect the slightest acquaintance on the road, and he would block his path, and instead of discussing weather or politics, as was his custom, would lead the talk on gently to the topic of America and of his son's presence there. After days and days of hopeless waiting, when a colourful airmail letter had arrived by post, he had almost felt the same joy as if Mali had come back. He hardly had the patience to read the instruction, "To open cut here," but thrust his finger in desperately and gashed the air letter until it split longitudinally, forcing him to piece it together like a jigsaw puzzle for deciphering. The message simply said, "Arrived. New York is big. The buildings are very tall, not like ours. Thousands of motor cars in the street. Food is difficult. I am in a hostel. Next week I go to school." Jagan read it with pleasure, although he was somewhat disturbed at the boy's mention of "school" rather than "college." It had arrived by the first post, and he sat in the hall bench and pored over it for nearly an hour, scanning every word and visualizing Mali in that enormous background. He could not keep the good news to himself. The first entrance open to him was the Truth Printing Works. Nataraj was at his desk, ever affable and welcoming visitors. The door was only half open, and when the light was blocked Nataraj looked up from his proofs and smiled, and immediately Jagan made the announcement: "Mali has reached—"

"Have you received a telegram?"

"Oh, no, he's prudent. Won't waste ten rupees when ten cents—any idea how much a cent is worth in our money?"

Nataraj made a rapid calculation. A dollar, equivalent to five rupees, seven rupees in the black market as one of his customers had told him, four rupees odd according to the Government, a hundred cents to a dollar . . . He gave up the attempt at multiplication and division and thought it best to change the subject.

"You will be getting your proofs very soon."

"Oh, yes, I know that once you take it up, you will get on with it. As you know, it's a contribution and a service, and not written for profit." After this statement, he switched over to America: "It's a place of enormous buildings and lots of motor cars. I hope the boy will have a room on the ground floor and not too high up."

"Our boys are very clever," said Nataraj, "and can take care of themselves anywhere in the world."

Accepting this agreeable statement, Jagan withdrew from the doorway and proceeded towards his shop. He caught a glimpse of the adjournment lawyer at the turning of Kabir Lane. He clapped his hands and stopped him. He could take that liberty with him as they had been classmates at the Albert Mission more than a generation ago and had been together in the National Movement (although the lawyer elegantly avoided going to prison). The lawyer, a one-toothed man with a sprinkling of silver dust on his unshaven cheeks, smiled, exposing his bare gums. "I've got to go home; some parties are waiting for me."

"I won't take more than a minute," said Jagan. "I felt you'd be happy to know that Mali has written."

"Have you received a telegram?"

What was the matter with everybody? Jagan felt annoyance at the tendency of people to get obsessed with telegrams. "After all, why spend ten rupees when ten cents bring over a letter in four days?"

"Four days!" said the lawyer. "No, no, you must be mistaken. It takes longer than that. It takes at least fifteen days."

That was the limit. How presumptuous of the man to talk of America, while he was there to provide first-hand information! People's notions were fixed. Stupid fellows. Frogs in the well!

Ahead of him, he saw the chemist at his door, looking down the street. He greeted Jagan warmly. "Rather late today?" he said with a lot of friendliness.

"Yes, I know, I know," Jagan said, approaching him eagerly. "The postman was rather late today. Well, when one has a son living so far away . . ."

"Has he reached America safely?"

"Yes, I was somewhat anxious for two or three days! Other boys would have wasted money on a telegram, but a letter at a tenth of the cost takes only a couple of days more. He's prudent, you know."

"What's the postage? I want to send for a free catalogue from Sears Roebuck. You know, it is an interesting book. It'll give us wonderful ideas on all sorts of things." Jagan almost groaned when the other asked, "What's the equivalent of fifty cents, which is the postage for the catalogue?"

He passed on. None so good as the cousin, who deserved

49

all the sweets he ate for his listening capacity: all the others in the town were obsessed with their own notions, were ignorant and resisted enlightenment on the subject of America. When he was in his seat, the head cook came to ask for the day's programme. Jagan repeated the formula and then added a postscript as a favour to the cook. "Mali has safely reached the other end, and that's a big relief to me. It's a huge country with a lot of motor cars. Everyone has a car there." The cook listened respectfully and turned away without comment. Jagan felt relieved that the fellow had not stopped to ask about telegrams or the equivalent of a cent.

He had to hold his soul in peace until four-thirty when the cousin arrived, passed straight in to savour, and came out of the kitchen. Jagan said with a quiet firmness, "The boy has reached the other end safely." He flourished a fragment of the air letter—as a special favour affording the cousin a glimpse of the letter, while he had only mentioned it to others.

"Excellent news! I knew he'd be all right," he said, smacking his lips.

"He didn't send a telegram."

"Yes, yes, why should he? Letters arrive so quickly nowadays. You must offer a couple of coconuts to Ganesha at the corner temple."

"Surely, it goes without saying," said Jagan, as if there were a specific contract between himself and the God in the matter of his son's safety. "It shall be done this very evening."

"I'll buy the coconut on my way," said the cousin, and immediately Jagan snatched up a coin from his drawer and handed it to the other.

"I feel a great burden off my head today. When someone

goes on such a long pilgrimage, especially if he is flying, it's always a worry, although one doesn't talk about it."

"I know, I know," said the cousin. "What does he say about himself?"

"He likes the new experience, of course. Lots of tall buildings and cars everywhere. I hope he will walk carefully in the streets. He says the food is good. I'm relieved. You know it's a country of millionaires. Everyone is so rich."

Mali proved unusually communicative from across the seas, and although at times he sounded brusque, disconnected, or impersonal, he generalized a good deal about the civilization in which he found himself. The blue airmail letters grew into a file. If only Mali had taken the precaution of leaving a proper margin to his epistles, Jagan would have bound them into a neat little volume at Truth Printing; surely Nataraj would have realized its importance and obliged him with a speedy execution. Jagan stuffed his jibba pocket with the letters and pulled them out for choice reading of passages to all and sundry, mostly to his cousin, who, as ever, remained an uncomplaining listener. Gradually his reading of the Bhagavad Gita was replaced by the blue airmail letters. From their study he formed a picture of America and was able to speak with authority on the subject of American landscape, culture, and civilization. He hardly cared or noticed whom he spoke to; anyone on the road seemed good enough. His acquaintances feared that he was afflicted with the talking disease.

From the minute he stepped out of his house he scanned the landscape for a familiar face, pounced hawklike on the unwary victim, and held him in thrall; he even stopped the vagrant on the culvert one day in order to describe the

Grand Canyon. "Actually, there is nothing like it anywhere in the world," he concluded and gave him five paise for listening. It was a matter of luck for another as to whether he could slip away in time or got entangled in American lore. Jagan found everyone restless when he spoke, but he rushed through his narration breathlessly. He had the feeling of having to bottle up his ideas until the blessed hour that brought in his cousin, who displayed such an enthusiasm for American information that Jagan could hardly tell him enough. The cousin often wanted to see the letters himself, but Jagan resisted the idea: he held them in sacred trust and could not allow a third person to touch them. Day after day, the cousin collected information on American life and manners and passed them on to his own circle of listeners. Very soon most people in Malgudi knew that fifty thousand human lives were lost in road accidents, every year, in America; and how people broke down on hearing of the death of Kennedy at street corners and crowded round anyone with a transistor radio. Jagan felt quite competent to describe, as if he had watched it himself, the route of Kennedy's motorcade on that fateful day, and he felt choked when he recounted how on that very morning, in Dallas, Kennedy had mingled in enormous crowds which grabbed and tore at his clothes and hair in sheer affection; nor did he spare his listener any detail of Oswald's death later.

The only letter Jagan rigorously suppressed was the one in which Mali had written, after three years' experience of America, "I've taken to eating beef; and I don't think I'm any the worse for it. Steak is something quite tasty and juicy. Now I want to suggest why not you people start eating beef? It'll solve the problem of useless cattle in our country and we won't have to beg food from America. I sometimes feel ashamed when India asks for American aid.

Instead of that, why not slaughter useless cows which wander in the streets and block the traffic?" Jagan felt outraged. The shastras defined the five deadly sins and the killing of a cow headed the list.

While he was cogitating on how to make his feelings felt on the subject and collecting quotations from the shastras and Gandhi's writings on the cow, to be incorporated in a letter to Mali, there came a cable one morning: "Arriving home: another person with me." Jagan was puzzled. What sort of a person? He had terrible misgivings and the added trouble of not being able to talk about it to the cousin, as he might spread the news of "another person" all over the town. His worst misgivings were confirmed on an afternoon when the train dumped Mali, "another person," and an enormous variety of baggage onto the railway platform and puffed away. The very sight of the streamlined suitcases and corded cartons filled Jagan with uneasiness and a feeling of inferiority. The old porter at the railway station could hardly handle this quantity of baggage, although normally he would seize and carry scores of boxes and baskets without a thought. Now he had to call in the boy at the cigarette shop for assistance. Mali kept muttering without moving his head or lips too much, "Be careful, awful lot of things that might break. Have spent a fortune in airfreight." Jagan slipped into the background, pushing his cousin to the fore to do all the talking and receiving. He was overwhelmed by the spectacle of his son, who seemed to have grown taller, broader, and fairer and carried himself in long strides. He wore a dark suit, with an overcoat, an airbag, a camera, and an umbrella on his person. Jagan felt that he was following a stranger. When Mali approached him extending his hand, he tried to shrink away and shield himself behind the cousin. When he had to speak to his son, with difficulty he restrained himself from calling him "sir" and employing the honorific plural.

Matters became worse when Mali indicated the girl at his side and said, "This is Grace. We are married. Grace, my dad." Complete confusion. Married? When were you married? You didn't tell me. Don't you have to tell your father? Who is she? Anyway she looks like a Chinese. Don't you know that one can't marry a Chinese nowadays? They have invaded our borders. . . . Or perhaps she is a Japanese. How was one to find out? Any indiscreet question might upset the gentleman with the camera. Jagan threw a panicky look at his cousin and fled on the pretext of supervising the loading of the baggage into Gaffur's taxi outside. A small gaping crowd followed them to the car murmuring, "He's come from America." Mali took notice of Gaffur by saying, "Jalopy going strong?" Gaffur did not understand the word "jalopy" (which sounded to everyone like the "jilebi" prepared in Jagan's shop). Jagan and the cousin sat with Gaffur in the front seat, leaving the back for Grace and Mali. Gaffur said without turning his head, "Why didn't you bring a car for me?" Jagan feared that Gaffur's familiarity might upset Mali, but the young man, fresh from democratic surroundings, said: "Wish you had told me; oh, I sold my Pontiac before leaving."

Gaffur, driving the car, entered into a description of the state of the nation with reference to automobiles—how you had to wait five years for a Fiat, three for an Ambassador, and so forth, and how no importation was allowed and how a brand-new Plymouth was seized and destroyed at the customs, all of which upset the young man, freshly come home.

Mali occasionally peeped out to say, "Nothing has changed."

Grace gazed with fascination at the streets and bazaars and cooed, "Oh, charming! Charming! Charming!"

"Honey, live in it and see what it is like," said Mali, on hearing which Jagan wondered whether he should really address her as Honey or Grace. When they approached the statue, she asked, "Who is that?" No one answered her question. Jagan became tense at the approach of the house beyond the statue. When they stopped he jumped out of the car and panted up the steps in order to open the main door. He had spent the fortnight in rigging up his house to suit his son's requirements. Under the guidance of the doctor's wife known to the cousin, he had spent a fortune in building a modern toilet and bathroom adjoining Mali's bedroom, and had scrubbed and colour-washed the walls and put up new tables and chairs. Mali went straight to his room to wash and change. Gaffur and the cousin left after piling the boxes in the passage. Grace was left alone, standing uncertainly in the hall. "Sit in that chair," Jagan said, unable to find anything else to say. He added, "Tell me what you want; I'll get it. I don't know what exactly you will like to have."

"Oh, how kind of you!" she said, genuinely pleased with his attention. She drew a chair for him and said, "Please be seated yourself; you must be tired."

"Oh, no," Jagan said. "I am a very active man. The whole secret of human energy . . ." he began, and cut short his sentence when he noticed a slight bewilderment in the girl's face. "I must really be off, you know, must go back to my shop, otherwise . . ."

"Oh, please do go and attend to your work. . . ."

"Make yourself comfortable," he cried from the passage and hurried out while Mali was still in the bathroom.

He began to avoid people. His anxiety was lest the lawyer or the printer or anyone else should stop him in the street to inquire about his daughter-in-law. He hurried on to his shop with downcast eyes. Even his cousin found great stretches of silence when they met. Jagan had grown unwilling to talk about his son. Everything about him had become an inconvenient question. The cousin wanted to know what Mali had qualified himself for, what he proposed to do, and above all, who was that casteless girl at home. He was dying to know what dietary arrangements were made at home and if they cooked meat. He inquired indirectly, "Does Mali still like our coffee or does he ask for tea as some of these foreign-returned people do?"

Jagan understood the purpose of this question and said, in order to put an end once and for all to inquisitiveness, "What another person eats or drinks never interests me; why should I pry into it? They have their kitchen, and they should know what to do with themselves."

"It'd be all right for Mali. But it's the girl I'm thinking of. . . ."

"Oh, she is all right. She was cooking for him and feeding him before and she is able to do it now, I suppose." Feeling suddenly that after all the cousin did deserve some enlightenment, he added, "I can only provide what I'm used to. If they don't like it, they can go and eat where they please."

"The Palace Hotel in the New Extension, I hear, provides European food."

"Whatever it is, one can only do one's duty up to a point. Even in the Gita, you find it mentioned. The limit of one's duty is well defined."

The cousin changed the subject: he'd agreed with so much of the Gita day after day that he felt weary of it. As long as Mali's blue airmail had been the theme, the Gita had receded into the background. Now it was coming back, which showed that Jagan was becoming mentally disturbed once again.

Occasionally one of Mali's old friends came to meet him. He seated the friend in the hall and conversed in low tones, as became a gentleman, and Jagan had no means of knowing what they talked about. Perhaps Mali was describing the Grand Canyon and the Niagara and the Statue of Liberty and the traffic jams in New York; he knew all about such things and could have joined in their talk if they'd let him, but he felt it might seem presumptuous unless he was invited. In that hope he sometimes let his feet lag crossing the hall while Mali was playing a gramophone or a tape-recorder or displaying to his friend a Polaroid camera or one or another of the hundred things he'd brought with him—which had included a wrapped package for Jagan. Grace had pressed it into his hands with: "Father, this is for you." It was a pale yellow casket with compartments containing spoons and forks and knives. He had examined it, turned it round in his hand and said, "Beautiful! But what is it?"

Grace replied, "It's a picnic hamper. Mali thought you would appreciate it."

"Of course, it's welcome," Jagan had said, wondering how one ever used it, and locked it up in his almirah.

Mali never wore a dhoti at home but a pair of dark trousers over a white shirt, and always had his feet in slippers. He hardly ever left his room or visited any other part of the house. He seldom went out; if he did, he waited for darkness to descend on the town and then dressed elaborately in socks, shoes, jacket, and tie, stepped out in the company of Grace, and strolled up a deserted part of New Extension Road, but never in the direction of the statue or Market Road. He carried himself like a celebrity avoiding the attention of the rabble.

One morning Grace parted the mustard-coloured curtain which divided the house into two sections, came into

Jagan's quarters, and tidied them up. He was not used to being helped and felt uneasy while his roll of mat was shaken and put away, and his pillow of hard cotton patted. She washed the vessels in his kitchen and arranged them neatly on a shelf. His protests went unheeded. She clutched the broom and raked every corner of the floor, saying, "Father, you think I mind it? I don't. I must not forget that I'm an Indian daughter-in-law." Jagan did not know what to say in reply and mumbled, "That's true indeed." She was stooping and scrubbing the ancient granite sink in the kitchen at floor level, tucking up her sari (which she had learnt to wear), and exposing her ivory-hued kneecap. Jagan could not take his eyes off that ivory patch as he protested, "Oh, Grace, Grace, you must not. I'm not used to it. Don't you bother yourself. I believe in doing all my work myself."

"And I believe in not letting you do it, that's all," she said. "I like to work. What else should I be doing all day?"

Jagan, who had been in the puja room, before the Gods, now followed her about, turning the rosary between his fingers. He said, "What will people think if they see a modern girl, brought up in New York, doing all this drudgery? Mali may not like it."

"It's not his business anyway," she said. "He is writing letters, and I'm doing the house, that's all. This is the loveliest house I have ever seen in my life."

"Don't you find it musty and old?"

"No, it's lovely. I've always dreamt of living in a house like this."

Nowadays he left home late, as he had got into the habit of waiting for Grace. He was getting used to the extreme air of orderliness that the feminine touch imparted to one's surroundings. One day Grace said, "I wish you would let me cook for you."

"Oh, that is impossible. I'm under a vow about that." He explained how he ate to live only on what he could cook with his own hands.

Grace cried, "Oh, you sound thrilling!" This was the first time someone had had a good word to say about his habits. Encouraged by her enthusiasm, he expatiated on his own creations of salt-free and sugar-free food, and concluded by saying that she should really look forward to reading his book when Truth Printing let it out of the press. She said ecstatically, "I'm sure it's going to be a best seller."

At the earliest chance he inquired, feeling very awkward, "What did Mali . . . I mean, what I want to ask is, has he finished his studies and acquired a degree in America?"

Grace looked up from a vessel she was scrubbing, and asked, "Why, didn't you know?"

Jagan now felt that he must cover up his relationship with his son and not betray the actual state of affairs, and so said, "I had no time actually to talk to Mali about these matters."

"Yes, yes, I understand," Grace said. "Still he ought to have told you."

"Oh, no," cried Jagan. "Don't take it that way. I am not complaining."

"Of course not," she agreed and said, "Still I say that Mali should have told you. Suppose I ask him to speak to you about it; it is pretty important, you know. Unless he talks to you, what can he plan, really?"

"Yes, I was also thinking so. I'd like to know his plans."

"You will, you will," she said.

Jagan said, "I thought he would mention something in his letters, but you know I only learnt a great deal about your country from them."

At this she rose to her feet with a peal of laughter, and

said, "Oh, oh, Father, Father, get me one of the letters and I will tell you something."

"What?" Jagan asked rather puzzled. "What do you mean?"

"Have you any of those letters? I will explain."

He went to his favourite cupboard and took out a cardboard box in which all the blue letters had been neatly treasured, and riffled through the lot. "Here they are, I do not know which one you want to see." He was still hesitant, being averse to letting anyone touch these valuable documents, but he could not say so to Grace.

"Wow! What a lot!" she exclaimed, and pulled out a letter at random. "Ah, here it is!" She pointed to the signature at the end. "Can you read this?"

Jagan fumbled for his glasses, put them on, and read aloud, " 'GM,' is it?"

"Surely, didn't you notice it before? I thought you knew. 'GM' is Grace and Mali, that's me and him, after we —we . . ." She trailed off. "I composed all those letters, though both of us signed them."

"You wrote them?" Jagan said, gulping down the saliva in his awkwardness. "How should I know? I never even knew that you were there."

"Didn't Mali ever write to you himself?"

Jagan remained silent. This was not going to do anyone any good; he silently prayed to Gandhi's spirit to forgive the lie he was about to utter. "Yes, yes; but I did not know these letters were yours."

"What did Mali have to say about me? Were you shocked?"

"He didn't describe you in detail. How can anyone write about a person fully? Words after all convey so little; that's why I thought he was taking up a very difficult line when he said he wanted to be a writer." He was rambling on thus when Grace put away her mop and brooms, came up, and sat down by his side, dangling her legs down the steps of the courtyard. "I didn't gather much about you from him." He let his clumsy imagination soar. "He only wrote that he was going to marry. I didn't know much about you; even now I don't know much about you except that you are a good girl."

"I suppose that is all one should bother about, don't you think? Why should we ask or know more?"

Jagan did not like to let this opportunity slip and said, "It is a custom in this country to inquire where one was born and bred and who is who generally, and then we go on to other things."

"Only the passport and income-tax people ask for such details in other countries. However, since I am also an Indian now, I might as well get used to things, and tell you something. My mother was a Korean and my father was an American soldier, serving in the Far East after the Second World War. I was born in New Jersey when my father went on home leave and took my mother along; he was recalled when my mother was still pregnant, and . . ." She remained silent for a moment and said, "He never came home again. . . . My mother decided to stay in America and I studied at Margaret's. Have you heard of it?"

"No," Jagan said. "What is it?"

"A girls' school. How I adore the memory of it!"

"Must be a good place," Jagan said out of his habit of picking up titbits of American information, and building on them.

"I studied domestic science at Michigan and met Mo when he came there for his creative writing course. We sat side by side at a football game; oh, you must see the football games in Michigan; do you have such things here?"

"Yes, yes, we have football too. All the schoolboys play it," Jagan said.

"I thought he must have written you all about it," she said.

"Yes, yes, but you know sometimes letters get lost. . . . The other day I heard a friend complaining to the post-master that his letters never reach him properly. . . ."

"You are happy, aren't you?" she asked suddenly. Jagan nodded. She said, "I had heard so much about the caste system in this country. I was afraid to come here, and when I first saw you all at the railway station I shook with fear. I thought I might not be accepted. Mo has really been wonderful, you know. It was very courageous of him to bring me here."

"Well, we don't believe in caste nowadays, you know," Jagan said generously; "Gandhi fought for its abolition."

"Is it gone now?" she asked innocently.

"It's going," Jagan said, sounding like a politician; "we don't think of it nowadays," hoping that the girl would not cross-examine him further.

Mali suddenly dashed into Jagan's presence one day to ask, "Can't you get a telephone for the house?"

Jagan said, "I've not thought of it."

"Yes, that's it. This is awkward and backward. How can we do any business without a telephone?"

Jagan wanted to say, "After all, Malgudi is a small town; everyone is within shouting distance."

"Even in your business," Mali went on, "if you had a telephone, more business would flow in. People might order by telephone."

Jagan merely said, "I've not thought of it," while he wanted to reply, "My daily sale is such and such even without a telephone, which shows that when one wants to eat sweets one doesn't wait for a telephone."

The boy said, "I felt embarrassed because I could not give my associates a telephone number."

"Who are your associates? What's the association?"

"Grace!" Mali called. "Will you join us? We are discussing business now."

Jagan was seized with a cold dread at the prospect of a business discussion with Mali, although pleased that after all Mali was going to talk to him. He was in one of his rare moods of communication. Jagan could see by the deliberate manner in which Grace kept herself in the background that she must have been responsible for this meeting. Mali suggested, "Father, let us adjourn to the hall. We have chairs there." Jagan was getting ready to leave for his shop but thought it worth while to postpone his routine. Nowadays, with one thing and another, his time-table was getting slightly upset.

Jagan obediently trooped behind his son, and took his seat in the hall, where he had not stepped for many weeks now. He noticed how Grace had transformed the place with curtains, mats, and tablecloth. A couple of modern paintings hung on the walls; Jagan found them bewildering, but said, "Yes," when Grace asked, "Aren't they marvellous?" The bamboo chairs were covered with coloured cushions. A little vase on a table held a sprig of tender margosa leaves. Jagan's heart throbbed at the sight. He said, "Margosa is the ambrosia mentioned in our Vedas, did you know that, Grace?"

She almost hugged the flower vase, and cried, "How grand! How did they know? They know all about everything in the Vedas, don't they?"

"Of course they do; all the Vedas have emanated from God's feet."

63

"Ah! What an idea!" Grace cried. She found everything thrilling. Everything stirred some poetic feeling deep within her.

Mali cautioned her, "Don't start swallowing margosa leaves, my dear."

Jagan said, "No harm in it. It is a natural antiseptic, purifies the blood, supplies iron." His eyes lit up when he spoke of margosa leaves. "I've explained it in detail in my book. When you read it, you will understand better. . . ." Grace was now readjusting the flowers in the vase with a deliberate interest, as if she were privileged to handle ambrosia as a result of marrying an Indian.

It was a long time since Jagan had observed his son's face at close quarters. Now he noticed that the freshness and the glow of foreignness that he had possessed when he arrived was gone; he looked even a shade below par. He had not reacquired the taste for South Indian food but ate his meals out of hermetically sealed tins. Jagan repressed his remarks on this subject, although he sadly noted the fact that Mali's eyes were dark-ringed. What was he worrying about? Jagan patiently waited for the other to speak. He noticed that Mali wore socks under his sandals, and wanted to cry out, "Socks should never be worn because they are certain to heat the blood through interference with the natural radiation which occurs through one's soles, and also because you insulate yourself against beneficial magnetic charges of the earth's surface. I have argued in my book that this is one of the reasons, a possible reason, for heart attacks in European countries." While he was busy with these thoughts, he was also dimly aware that Mali had been talking; he had been aware of the sound, but he had missed the substance of the words. He had anticipated this meeting for a long time, and he realized now with a shudder that he had probably missed the opportunity of a lifetime. He woke up with a start and became extra attentive, bending to the task all his powers of concentration, as Mali was concluding his passage with, "You get it?"

Jagan was at a loss whether to say "Yes" or "No," but sat staring ahead and making noncommittal sounds in his throat.

"Well, think it over; you have all the data," said Mali. Then he glanced at his watch and rose muttering, "I must check at the rail station about my unaccompanied baggage, expected today; if only we had a telephone . . ." He went to the door, turned to Grace, and said, "Don't wait for lunch." They heard his scooter palpitating away.

Jagan sat still, quietly enjoying the thought that his son had spoken to him at such length. When he rose to go, Grace held the door open for him and asked, "Did you have any questions for Mali? Was everything clear?"

Jagan replied, "I can always go back to the subject, can't I?" with a significant smile, and Grace said, "Of course."

Chapter Six

The cousin nowadays found Jagan rather hesitant to speak about his son, but on the theory that conversation must go on, he said, "Did you hear that there was a fight at the market? The jaggery merchant as usual was cornering the stock, and . . ."

Jagan, seated on his throne, with the scent of frying ghee filling the hall, said, "Our merchants are becoming heartless."

"You just wait and see what's going to happen to the rice dealers; they are playing with fire."

"Even when one wants to make profits, one should retain some sense of service. I have not raised the price here, in spite of the sugar crisis."

"Oh, everybody is not you," the cousin flattered, giving a soft back stroke to his tuft. Flattery was his accredited business in life; even when he joked and disparaged it was all a part of his flattery. "You are not one who knows how to make money. If you were unscrupulous, you could have built many mansions, who knows?"

"And what would one do with many mansions?" asked Jagan, and quoted a Tamil verse which said that even if eighty million ideas float across your mind, you cannot wear more than four cubits of cloth or eat more than a little measure of rice at a time.

"Ah!" jeered the cousin genially, stuffing a piece of to-bacco into his mouth, "that's why I say that you do not know the art of living and flourishing, and yet the goddess of wealth chooses you for her favours!"

Jagan laughed happily, and feeling that the other now deserved a little dose of information about Mali, said, "I came late this morning because Mali wanted to discuss his plans." He was very proud of being able to mention something so concrete about his son.

The cousin became alert and sat up attentively in order not to miss a word. Jagan paused after the announcement and the cousin filled the momentary gap with, "I had a glimpse of him this morning on a scooter. Has he bought one?"

"It's a friend's, I hear. He must have a conveyance."

"Who could that friend be?" the cousin speculated. "Scooter-riding boys—one is that kerosene agent's son; another is the man who has come from the Punjab to establish a button factory. Another scooter belongs to the District Judge's nephew—you know that young man in the Public Works Department in charge of the new roads in the hills. . . ."

"Boys must have their own vehicles nowadays; they don't like to walk," generalized Jagan.

"I always like to move on my feet, but these are days of speed; people must go from place to place quickly. They have more to do than we had. Don't you think so?"

"Mali has never fancied walking. He has always cycled. I bought him his first bicycle when he was seven years old, and he could go wherever he pleased. I sometimes found that he would cycle up to Ellaman Street, not in the least minding the crowd at Market Road."

"Even adults shy away from Market Road in the evenings."

"But that boy grew up fearlessly, full of self-reliance at an age when other boys of his age were being mollycoddled."

"But, poor boy, his mother was so ailing."

"That's another reason why I tried to keep his mind diverted."

The dialogue was rambling off into a series of side issues. The cousin now tried to pull it back to the main theme. "You were starting to tell me about Mali's plans. You must be feeling relieved now."

"Yes, yes, but I always knew that everything must be going well, with nothing to bother about."

"Now, have you any idea of his plans?"

"Yes, yes. He was in a hurry to go to the railway station this morning, and he could give me only a general idea. Of course, he'll tell us the details later." This was the utmost Jagan could essay without betraying his ignorance.

The cousin asked abruptly, "Are you in favour of his scheme?"

"Which scheme?" Jagan asked, looking surprised. He hadn't suspected any scheme. The cousin paused for a second, while the noise of school breaking up next door enlivened the air. A group of children as usual hung about the front stall gazing at the sweets arranged on trays. "Captain, don't allow crowds to stand there; they obstruct the traffic." Traffic was not Jagan's real concern—there were many obstructions on Market Road; a couple of cows belonging to a milk-seller always stood in the centre of the road in their off-hours, not to speak of a rogue bull belonging to no one in particular, which sometimes chased the cows amorously, scattering pedestrians, jutkas, and cycles alike onto the steps of the shops; there were groups from villages bringing in grain and fruit to the market who clogged the edge of Market Road in a circle overflowing onto the middle. Cycles and bullock carts and automobiles threaded their way through without damage to themselves; no one protested or bothered. But Jagan always mentioned the word "obstruction" because the sight of the children at the counter made him uneasy, or even guilty at times. He preferred them to go away without looking at the sweets so hungrily. It was also his habit to call out the captain and issue an order whenever he felt any sort of mental strain.

The cousin now realized that the word "scheme" was setting up an agitation in Jagan's mind. He watched Jagan's face with satisfaction. Jagan's studied avoidance of the subject of his son had not been to the cousin's liking. It made him feel that he had been suddenly converted into an outsider; he didn't like the status, and so here he found an opportunity to bring himself back into the fold. "I didn't want to speak to you unnecessarily about it, but I'm so happy that the boy still calls me 'Uncle' whenever he meets me; although he has travelled to the other end of the earth, he has not forgotten his uncle. You see, I didn't like to thrust myself on him after his return home. People change, you know, especially when they go abroad. I know of a foreign-returned I.C.S. officer who disowned his parents when they came to meet him at the railway station."

"Horrible fellow, he must have been mad. Mali could not be in the least like him."

"I know, I know; that's what I am telling you now. I went to the Registrar's house last week, and Mali was talking to his son. You know their house at the New Extension? I'd gone there because I'd promised to find a suitable cook for them; the lady is not in good health. I have to do various things for various persons."

"The Registrar's son and Mali are friends, I suppose?"

"Oh, yes, they were conversing on the front veranda. As I passed in, Mali himself addressed me: 'Give me a few minutes before you go.' 'Yes, Mali,' I said; 'I'm at your service.' After finishing my business I came out and Mali said, 'I'll walk with you.' "

"Did he want to walk? I thought he never cared to walk."

"Only up to the gate, because he did not like to let his friends overhear what he wanted to say."

"What did he say?" Jagan asked, now completely at the mercy of the cousin.

"He wants to manufacture story-writing machines," said the cousin.

Jagan felt so baffled by this statement that he couldn't phrase his surprise properly. He blurted out a couple of questions incoherently and lapsed into silence.

The cousin watched his face, relishing the bewilderment he saw in it, and said with an innocent look, "Haven't you heard of story-writing machines?" as if they were an article of daily use. This was a piece of minor victory for him in the matter of American knowledge. Jagan felt it best to acknowledge defeat and give up all pretence. The cousin rubbed it in by saying, "I thought he would have told you everything. What else was he telling you this morning?"

Jagan said loftily, "We had other things to talk about. He was telling me of other matters."

"But this proposition is uppermost in his mind; he has been thinking of it night and day."

"Yes, yes," said Jagan. "I knew of course that he was speaking about a machine, but something else came up before I could ask him to explain."

"This is not just an ordinary machine," said the cousin. At this moment Jagan let out his periodic shout: "Captain! Why is there a crowd?" but the cousin continued in a tone of authority, "Now listen carefully. This story-writing machine, as you might have guessed, is a story-writing machine."

"How does it do that?" asked Jagan, genuinely surprised.

"Don't ask me," said the cousin. "I am not an engineer. Mali constantly used the word 'electronic' or 'electric' or something like that, and explained it at length. It sounds very interesting; why don't you ask him? I am sure he will be able to explain it to you satisfactorily."

Jagan bided his time, and the next morning, when Grace came in to clean his kitchen, applied for an interview. "I want to talk to Mali; is he free?"

"Of course," she said, "if he isn't, he will free himself for your sake." She paused and they heard the clatter of a type-writer from Mali's room. "He is busy, I think," she added. "I will tell him." She went up and came out a few minutes later with an air of importance. "He will see you in fifteen minutes."

For a moment Jagan felt as if he were a petitioner in his own house, and there flashed across his mind those far-off days when Mali used to stand at his door, cringing for some concession or for cash, and for a brief second he was aghast at the transformations that had come with time. "I have to be off myself," he said to redress the balance of importance, but Grace went back to her work in the kitchen without a reply. Unable to make up his mind, he idly opened a cup-board and stood gazing at the old bottles and packing pa-per that he had preserved on the theory of keeping a thing for seven years. Grace said from the kitchen, "Another day I will clean up that cupboard for you. We need to do some spring cleaning in this house."

Jagan, aghast at the implications, said with some inten-sity, "Don't do anything yet." Meanwhile the typewriter ceased and a bell sounded, and Grace said, "He is ready for you. You want to go in?" She seemed to have built up Mali into a celebrity. She led him forward. "He is very methodical, you know." Jagan was pleased and baffled at the same time. He girt himself for the interview. He glanced at the clock on the wall and muttered, "Must be going in fifteen minutes."

Jagan took the visitor's chair, looked for a brief moment at his son, and plunged into the subject straight away. "How exactly does the story-machine operate?"

"I explained it to you yesterday," said Mali.

"There were some points which I did not quite grasp, but I was in a hurry."

The son looked pityingly at him, rose, opened a packing case, pushed aside a lot of brown paper and thread, and lifted out a small object which looked like a radio cabinet and placed it on the table. "I was only waiting for this to arrive; yesterday I had to clear it from the railway office. What a lot of time is wasted here! I have never seen a more wasteful country than ours." Jagan refrained from retorting, "We find it quite adequate for our purposes." Now Mali stood beside the cabinet in the attitude of a lecturer; he patted it fondly and said, "With this machine anyone can write a story. Come nearer, and you will see how it works."

Jagan obediently pushed his chair back, rose, and stood beside his son, who seemed to tower above him. He felt proud of him. "God knows what he eats out of those tins; he looks tired, no doubt, but how well grown is he!" he reflected as Mali explained.

"You see these four knobs. . . . One is for characters, one for plot situations, the other one is for climax, and the fourth is built on the basis that a story is made up of character, situations, emotion, and climax, and by the right combination . . ."

He interrupted his oration for a moment to pull a drawer out and glance at a cyclostyled sheet of paper; he shut the drawer and came back to say, "You can work on it like a typewriter. You make up your mind about the number of characters. It works on a transistor and ordinary valves. Absolutely foolproof. Ultimately we are going to add a little fixture by which any existing story could be split up into components and analysed; the next model will incorporate it."

Jagan asked, "Do you want to use this for writing stories?"

"Yes, I am also going to manufacture and sell it in this country. An American company is offering to collaborate. In course of time, every home in the country will possess one and we will produce more stories than any other nation in the world. Now we are a little backward. Except *Ramayana* and *Mahabharata*, those old stories, there is no modern writing, whereas in America alone every publishing season ten thousand books are published." He rushed back to his desk and gazed on the cyclostyled sheet again before repeating, "Yes, ten thousand titles. It is a must for every home; all a writer will have to do is to own one and press the keys, and he will get the formula on a roll of paper, from which he can build up the rest. . . ."

Jagan left his seat and went over to examine the machine as if it were something ejected from another planet. He approached it so cautiously that Mali said, "Touch it and see for yourself." Jagan peered at the apparatus closely and read the headings: "Characters: good, bad, neutral. Emotions: love, hate, revenge, devotion, pity. Complexities: characters, incidents, accidents. Climax: placement and disposal, and conclusion." It looked pretty; its mahogany veneer was grained; its keys were green, red, and yellow to indicate the different categories.

"How can one write a story with it?" Jagan asked.

"Exactly as one does with a typewriter," Mali answered, and Jagan admired him for the fund of information he had gathered on the subject.

Just at this moment, Grace came in, stood beside them, and said, "Isn't he clever?" in a jocular manner. Jagan could not answer her immediately; his mind was too full of confusion and questions. He felt hemmed in: the room had lost its original appearance and looked like an office in a foreign country. What was Mali trying to do? What was his own part in all this activity? What was going to be the nature of his involvement? He said with some trepidation, "Grace, do you know that our ancestors never even wrote the epics? They composed the epics and recited them, and the great books lived thus from generation to generation in the breath of the people."

Before he could proceed further Mali said with a gesture of disgust, "Oh, these are not the days of your ancestors. Today we have to compete with advanced countries not only in economics and industry, but also in culture." While on the one hand Jagan felt delighted at the way his son seemed to be blossoming after years of sullen silence, he was at the same time saddened by the kind of development he noticed in him now. The boy went on, "If you have the time, I'd like to explain to you one or two other points." Jagan helplessly glanced at a travelling clock on Mali's table, and jingled the keys of his shop in the depths of his jibba pocket. "Ultimately, you may have to give up your sweet-making and work in our business. I'll give you a nice air-conditioned room with a couple of secretaries."

Jagan had never known his son could talk so fluently; he wished secretly that he would speak differently. He felt the time had come for him to ask his questions. "Do they write all their stories with this machine in America?" he asked, as if he wished to fill a lacuna in his knowledge of that land and its civilization.

"Mostly, mostly," said Mali.

"Most magazines," added Grace, "are nowadays switching over to the machine in their fiction departments, and out of the best sellers last year at least three were a product of it."

"The proposition is that we get American collaboration worth two hundred thousand dollars, provided we find fifty-one thousand to start the business," said Mali.

"Fifty-one thousand dollars would be the equivalent of . . ." began Jagan, starting the age-old calculation.

"Work it out yourself," said Mali with a touch of irritation in his voice. "Let me first finish my sentence. They will be responsible for the know-how and technical personnel, help us set up the plant, run it for six months, and then quit; they will also provide us with promotional material." What a lot of new expressions the boy had learnt, Jagan reflected with admiration, while Mali added, "We shall have to collect forty-nine thousand dollars by public subscription, and the controlling stock will be in our hands."

Jagan had thought till then that his son was a moron. He looked for a brief second at Grace and asked, "What was your subject in the college?" She answered, "I've told you I graduated in domestic economy at Michigan."

"Why go into all that now?" asked Mali.

Jagan said, rising, "I was wondering if Grace had also studied business subjects." And now it was Mali's turn to wonder why his father said that.

Jagan left without further comment.

At four-thirty, when the cousin arrived, he told him, "Have you any idea what fifty thousand dollars is in rupees?"

The cousin said, "A little over two lakhs of rupees."

"How do you know?"

"By a simple calculation, and I also verified it yesterday when I met Dodhaji, our banker, after I left Mali."

"Two lakhs!" mused Jagan. "Where does one find it?"

"In your bank book," said the cousin promptly in a jocular way.

"Are people under the impression that I have amassed wealth?"

"Yes, of course, although everyone admires your simple living and high-thinking habits."

"How can wealth accumulate with the price of foodstuff standing where it is? I just keep up the business so that these poor fellows may not be thrown out of employment, that's all."

"That everybody knows," said the cousin. "Are you interested in buying raisins? I saw a fresh stock arrive at the sait's shop; hand-picked quality."

"Have you asked the cook?"

"He told me that he needed them because I found sohan papdi rather tame without raisins today."

Jagan cried furiously, "Is that so? Why didn't he tell me?"

The cousin said, "You didn't come in time, that's all, and he couldn't wait for the stuff. Why do you get upset?"

"It's because I do not like the idea of cheating my customers. Do you realize that the price for the customer remains the same with or without raisins?"

"And your own margin of profit is improved," said the cousin. Jagan glared at him. The cousin added, "You are a rare being, but that would be the only line of thought of some of your compatriots in this city."

Mollified, Jagan said, with a touch of pride, "I was held

up by Mali, poor boy. I have to give him the time he needs now and then; otherwise there is bound to be a lot of mis-understanding. His ideas turn on big figures nowadays. He seems to have learnt many things in America."

"He wants me to use my influence to sell the shares of the company."

This was a big relief to Jagan. "I'm sure many people will be interested in the proposal."

"Including your goodself."

"No harm in finding five or ten along with the rest."

"Mali's idea is different. He has reserved five or ten for people outside, and counts on you for the fifty-one thou-sand dollars for a start."

"And you have found its rupee equivalent?"

"About two and a half lakhs of rupees."

"Where does one find it?"

"I've already indicated . . ."

"Does Mali think so?"

"Of course, and he also says he knows where you keep cash not sent to the bank."

"He says so, does he?" said Jagan, laughing within him-self at the fact that he had changed the venue of the im-maculate cash. "Money is an evil," he added with great feeling.

The cousin said, "Shall I ask the front-stall boy to throw away that bronze jug?"

They both laughed at the joke, but the relaxation was short-lived for Jagan. He became very serious suddenly and said, "I hope you will find an occasion to tell my son that I have not got all that money."

"Now you are both on speaking terms, why don't you tell him yourself?"

Jagan sighed and said, "I do not wish to spoil his mood."

The tempo of Mali's demands increased. Though at one time Jagan had sighed for a word from his son, he now wished that the thaw had not occurred.

He was being hunted. When he passed in and out of the house he felt his steps were watched, his face being secretly studied for a "Yes" or "No." Grace gazed at his face meaningfully. Mali, if he was at home, kept coming into his quarters on some excuse or other. After the first day's demonstration Jagan studiously avoided all literary topics. "Here is a scheme to make me a bankrupt," he said to himself whenever he heard footfalls approaching his room. "Fifty-one thousand dollars! I am not growing overfond of money; but I'm not prepared to squander it. Why should we want stories or machines for writing them?"

One morning Mali stood at the doorway of the puja room after his breakfast, in blue pants, with his hand resting on the top of the threshold as Jagan sat before his Gods. "They do everything with machines nowadays. Washing machines —have you seen one?"

"No," said Jagan, trying to cut all mechanical references to a minimum.

"Grinding, powdering, or calculating—nowadays one uses electricity for everything." Behind him stood Grace, who added, "Even for sharpening pencils we have machines."

"We should have brought one with us," Mali said, turning to her. Mali, who never used to seek him before, was now intruding even into the privacy of his puja room, interrupting his prayers. Jagan met this disturbance passively—by shutting his eyes and muttering some incantations until Grace said, "We should not disturb his prayers." Prayer was a sound way of isolating oneself—but sooner or later it ended: one could not go on praying eternally, though one ought to.

He had become rather sneaky nowadays. Soon after his prayers, he tiptoed to the kitchen to prepare his salt-free food, bolt it down, put on his khadi jibba, and slip away with the least noise, but he always found Grace at the passage ready to open the door for him with some remark about the weather or politics, gazing on his face with an unmistakable inquiry about his views on the machine. He was amazed at the intensity of her interest in Mali's fortunes. As ever, he had two opposite feelings: appreciation of her interest in Mali and resentment at her effort to involve him in their business. Mali never thrust himself forward more than a minimum; he seemed to have left the task to Grace; even his visitation at the threshold of the puja room in the mornings seemed to have been dictated by Grace. An occasional misgiving tainted Jagan's thoughts—might not Grace's interest, friendliness, and attentiveness be a calculated effort to win his dollars?

As he walked to his shop with his head bowed in thought, when the vagrant at the statue corner greeted him and begged for money Jagan paused to ask, for the hundredth time in a year, "You are sturdy; why don't you seek work?"

"Where have I the time, master?" he said. "By the time I go round begging and return here the day is over."

Jagan tossed a five-paise coin at him, remembering an ancient injunction: "Perform thy charity without question."

In appreciation the beggar said, "Master does not tell me much about America nowadays. Why?"

"Because I have told you all that you should know."

"What's the little master doing?" asked the beggar, dogging his steps.

"Well, he'll be starting a factory soon," replied Jagan, without conviction.

"What'll he make?"

"Some machinery," Jagan said, not wishing to elaborate

79

and wishing the beggar would leave him alone. Fortunately he slipped off to pester some other person coming in the opposite direction, and Jagan quickened his pace. Passing Truth Printing, he spied Nataraj alone at his desk, and on an impulse stopped to ask, "I hope you have not forgotten my work?"

"How could I?" said Nataraj. "As soon as the pressure of the seasonal printing lessens, yours will be the first. I'm your family printer, you know. Your son has given me some urgent work which he wants in three days, the prospectus for his new enterprise."

"Ah!" cried Jagan. The "scheme" seemed to dog his steps.

"Your name is in it!" said Nataraj.

"Ah! Ah!" exclaimed Jagan.

Nataraj pushed up his rolltop and produced a proof sheet on which Jagan saw his name in print as one of the principal promotors of Mali Enterprises. The others in the list were Grace and a few of Mali's scooter-riding friends.

Nataraj studied his face and said, "Why, aren't you pleased?"

Jagan replied in a hollow tone: "Yes, yes, no doubt."

"Seems to be an interesting new kind of enterprise."

"Yes, yes, no doubt."

He hurriedly left for his shop. As the cook stood before him taking instructions for the day, he feared he too might begin to speak of the story-writing machine, but luckily this man's universe of kitchen smoke and frying oil had not lost its insularity yet. Occupying his throne, with the scent of incense and frying, Jagan recovered a little bit of his sense of security. He opened the drawer and let his eyes rest on the copy of the Bhagavad Gita for a while, opened a page at random, and tried to get absorbed in its eternal message, but a part of his mind was deeply injured by the sight of his own name in print on the prospectus. How could Mali perpetrate such a deed, take so much for granted? But the poor boy probably had complete confidence in his father's support, and there was nothing heinous in that. It was quite natural. Still, he should at least have had the courtesy to mention it to him. Neither Grace nor Mali . . . But perhaps they had been hanging about his puja room to inform him of that rather than ask for capital; and he blamed himself for not giving them a chance.

Whoever the American associate was, he had done his coaching perfectly; and Nataraj also proved extraordinarily prompt. The city was soon flooded with the prospectus of Mali's company. The first one came by post to Jagan himself at his shop. It went into the cultural shortcomings of the country, and the need for it to take its place in the comity of nations, and how this machine was going to cut time and distance and lift the country out of its rut, and then followed many facts and figures. One thing Jagan noted was that the jungles on Mempi Hills would provide the soft wood required for some part of the machine, and it could be had for a song. Then it went into details of production and marketing and location. Jagan now realized that the son of the kerosene agent was actually the economic brain behind the whole show—a young fellow in jeans and striped shirt who rode a scooter and carried Mali on the pillion seat.

Very soon they abandoned the scooter and were seen moving about in an old automobile. Grace explained to Jagan one morning, "The company have now made a start with an automobile. Although it's an old one, it is useful. One has to move about so much on business, nowadays."

"What car is it? It looks green," said Jagan, out of the polite need to say something, and not wishing to ask, "What is its price? Who has paid for it?"

Grace replied, "It's pretty, isn't it?" and Jagan lapsed into meditation before the Gods, and remained in meditation until she moved away from the threshold and he could hear her talking to Mali in the front portion of the house.

"Gandhi has taught me peaceful methods, and that's how I'm going to meet their demand. These two are bent upon involving me in all sorts of things," he reflected. He was bewildered by his son's scheme and distrusted it totally. He was aware that pressure was being subtly exercised on him to make him part with cash. He was going to meet the situation by ignoring the whole business; a sort of non-violent non-cooperation.

But he found his domestic life irksome. He had lost the quiet joy of anticipation he used to experience whenever he turned the statue corner. He felt nervous as he approached the ancient house. The expectant stare of Grace when she opened the door, and the significant side-glances of Mali, got on his nerves. He was aware of a silent tension growing. He felt happy if nobody came when he turned the key in the door, as at the times when both of them were away, Grace shopping, and Mali with his local associates in his green car. Thank God, Jagan thought, for the green car. When he was in, if he heard them open the front door, he retreated far into the back yard of the house or sometimes even locked himself in the bathing shack.

But the state of non-cooperation could not last forever. Grace asked him one morning point-blank, "Have you thought over the proposition?"

Jagan felt cornered—if he had just picked up his upper cloth a minute earlier, he could have reached the street by now. Grace had studied his movements and timed her interception perfectly. He had dodged this encounter for two weeks by sheer manœuvring of arrival and departure.

Now he felt trapped. He wanted to say, "Leave these questions for menfolk to settle; keep away, you charmer from Outer Mongolia or somewhere." She had stuck a flower with a pin in her bobbed hair and he longed to tell her, "Take off that flower, it's ridiculous." He merely remarked, "I see that you have jasmine in your hair this morning."

"As it's a Friday, I have remembered my duties as a Hindu wife. I have also washed the doorsteps and decorated the threshold with white flour. I went to a shop yesterday to get it. See what I have done!" She was so importunate that he had to look cheerful and follow her out. She pointed at a floral design on the ground and cried, "Don't you believe now that I could have been a Hindu in my last life? I am able to bend down and draw the design on the floor as I see a lot of others do."

Jagan wanted to say, "An orthodox Hindu woman would never clip her hair as you have done," but actually remarked, "It's a long time since anyone attended to these things in this house. How did you know that Friday is auspicious?"

"I have friends who tell me what is proper," she said.

Just as Jagan was thinking of slipping away, a window opened; Mali peeped out and commanded, "Father, come in for a moment. I must talk to you." Jagan felt that Grace had only been holding him in a trap and scowled at her accusingly; but she merely said, as though she were the usherette at a Presidential interview, "Certainly, go in," suggesting that he should feel honoured at the summons.

Muttering, "I have to go and open the shop," Jagan went in. Mali was at his desk and flourished a finger towards the visitor's chair. Jagan lowered himself into it gingerly, still muttering, "I must go and open the shop."

Mali ignored his plea and asked, "Have you thought it over?"

"What?" asked Jagan, trying to look absent-minded, but he knew he was not bringing it off successfully, for Grace, sneaking up behind as if to complete her trapping operations, held him in a pincer movement. Mali tossed a prospectus at him. "I mailed you one, didn't you get it?" Jagan said neither yes nor no; there was danger in either statement, but his mind wandered off in another direction: how could Nataraj have managed to issue this piece of work so quickly from his press, while his own book remained untouched for so many years? What charm did Mali exercise? As he sat brooding on it, Mali suddenly said, "You don't even care to look at it."

Jagan feared that the season of sweet temper was coming to a close, and replied mildly, "I have looked at it, and I have also noticed that you have put my name in without even telling me."

"What is happening to you? On the very first day I spoke to you, I spent over thirty minutes in explanations; I asked if I might print your name and didn't you say 'Go ahead'?"

Jagan cast his mind back. "What day was that?"

Mali's temper had now risen. Grace saw the symptoms and stepped in to say, "On the very first day when he explained his scheme . . ."

"Oh, yes, of course yes," said Jagan, realizing that he could have said anything at any time. He added mildly, "Yes, but I naturally thought you would tell me again before actually going to press, you know."

"I really do not know what you mean. You expect everything to be said ten times; no wonder nothing gets done in this country."

"Why do you blame the country for everything? It has been good enough for four hundred millions," Jagan said, remembering the heritage of the *Ramayana* and the Bha-

gavad Gita and all the trials and sufferings he had undergone to win independence. He muttered, "You were not
born in those days."

Mali made a gesture of despair. "I do not know what
you are talking about. I want to get on with our business.
We had two long sessions, and I told you everything, and
now—" Grace interposed to say, "Father, if you have any
questions, I am sure Mali will be glad to answer them."

Jagan felt, like a man in a witness box, that anything he
uttered might be used as evidence against him. He said, "I
must be going now, I have to open the shop."

Mali said, "We have to make a beginning, our associates
are waiting on us. We will lose everything unless we act at
once. I have explained to you the basis of our participation."
Fifty thousand dollars! Whatever its equivalent might be, it
was a staggering sum.

"I am a poor man," Jagan wailed, and immediately noticed the shock on Mali's face and the embarrassment he
had created before Grace. It was as if he had uttered a bad
word. Seeing this, Jagan said, "Gandhi always advocated
poverty and not riches."

"And yet you earn your thousand rupees a day, or what
is it?" asked Mali with a vicious smile.

"If you feel you can take up the business and run it, do
so; it is yours if you want it."

"You expect me to do that? I have better plans than to be
a vendor of sweetmeats."

Jagan did not wait to hear more. He pushed the chair
back very slowly and gently, pausing for a second to study
the faces of the other two. For once he saw Grace's eyes
unlit with a smile. It was impassive. "Is she a good girl or a
bad one?" Jagan asked within himself. "I wish I could decide." Mali was biting his thumbnail and kicking the foot-

rest below the table. Jagan did not have the courage to stay and face him. Without another word, he took his upper cloth off the hook and was out of the room in a moment.

When he passed the culvert at the confluence the vagrant said, "My master does not even look at me nowadays."

"I gave you five paise only . . ." He couldn't remember when, but he concluded, "I am a poor man like you. Do you think I have inexhaustible cash?"

The vagrant said, "Master should not say such a thing."

At least this fellow spoke better than Mali, in similar circumstances, who didn't want him if he did not claim to be a wealthy father.

He remained morose throughout the day. At four-thirty the cousin entered the kitchen and came out. He sensed that Jagan was waiting to spring some terrible information on him. Wiping his lips with the towel, he sat down on his stool, remarking, "Chandra Kala [Crescent of the Moon] tastes absolutely divine today, and if the reputation of this shop is going to shoot sky-high in this town, it will be on account of it."

As always, flattery helped; a few webs spread around Jagan's eyes and he said, "It is purity that is important. Yesterday I came early to see that pure cow's butter was melted for frying. I won't touch buffalo butter, though it may be cheaper. Gandhi was opposed to buffalo products. I had sent one of the cooks to collect cow's butter from Koppal, he came back at five in the morning, and I came straight in before eight in order to melt it right. A fortune had been spent on it, and I didn't want to risk overboiling it."

"You pay attention to every detail. I have often wanted to ask you, why did you choose this business? Rather a specialized job, isn't it?"

"When I was in jail I was given kitchen duties, and after coming out this seemed to me as good a business as any other." He was slipping into a reminiscent mood, much to the relief of the cousin. "But the reputation of the shop is all due to Sivaraman; but for him I don't know where I would be. I wanted to serve the public in my own way by making available pure sweets, particularly for poor children."

"An excellent ideal," said the cousin, deliberately refraining from the reminder that poor children were just the ones who could not afford to buy sweets. He also said it another way. "If the stuff is to be pure a price has to be paid for it."

"That's true," said Jagan. He sat brooding for a while and then announced, "From tomorrow the price of everything will be reduced. I have made up my mind about it."

"Why?" asked the cousin in consternation.

Jagan spurned an explanation. He just said, "We buy provisions for, let us say, a hundred rupees a day, and the salaries of our staff and the rent amount to, let us say, a hundred," he lowered his voice, "and the stuff produced need not earn more than, let us say, two hundred in all. Now, the truth is . . ." he began, but slurred over the details at the last minute, not wishing to reveal the actual figures. "More people will benefit by a reduction."

"But you are opposed to the eating of sugar, aren't you?"

Jagan took time to digest this contradiction before saying, "I see no connection. If others want to eat sweets, they must have the purest ones, that is all. I am thinking particularly of children and poor people."

"What about your share?" the other asked testily.

"I have enough," Jagan said.

The cousin sought further explanation like someone

scrutinizing and assaying a tricky diplomatic statement. "Enough of what?" he asked.

"Of everything," Jagan said.

The cousin looked appropriately serious and gloomy. "If you are thinking of retiring from the business I am sure someone will be willing to take it over and run it."

"Oh, it is not so easy," Jagan said. "I told Mali so this morning and he said . . ." He remained silent. The recollection of the scene, he felt, would overwhelm him; he might break down and it would be silly to be seen in tears while he was occupying the throne. He had a mental picture of himself standing like a ragged petitioner in the presence of Mali and the Chinese girl, being sneered at for his business of a lifetime, a business that had provided the money for Mali to fly to America and do all sorts of things there. Vendor of sweetmeats, indeed! Jagan became aware of the cousin waiting for his reply and said quickly, "He was not interested in vending sweets."

The cousin felt that this was the right time to sound sympathetic and said, "What better income could one have? But, you see, his ideas are different, as you know."

"Money is an evil," Jagan said, uttering an oft-repeated sentiment. "We should all be happier without it. It is enough if an activity goes on self-supported; no need to earn money, no need to earn money. Captain!" he shouted. "Who are those boys? What do they want?"

"I will send them away, sir."

"No, no, tell that boy at the counter to give them each a packet and then send them away."

"They may not have the money."

"Who cares? I can afford to give away, boy," he shouted from his throne. "Treat those children." The children got their sweets and went away greatly surprised.

"If these boys go out and tell others, you will be mobbed and unable to leave the place."

"We will manage, don't worry," said Jagan. "In a day or two some changes are coming."

The cousin looked scared and said, "Don't be hasty, go out on a pilgrimage to the temples and bathe in the sacred rivers. I will mind the shop, if you like, while you are away."

"I will tell you when I am ready."

The boy from the front stall now brought in the bronze jug. The cousin, who usually timed his departure at this point, got up but did not leave, curious to know whether Jagan would accept the cash or just throw it out. Jagan pulled out the drawer, spread the folded towel to deaden the noise of coins cascading down, looked up at the cousin, and said, "Tonight and tomorrow I will have to do a lot of reckoning with concentration. I have left things to drift too long." The cousin, worrying where these hints were leading, said, like the peacemaker he was, "I will speak to Mali; I know I can talk to him. Even to that girl Grace, she is so trusting!"

"By all means, speak to him on any matter you like," Jagan said, and added with firmness, "But not on my behalf."

Chapter Seven

Two days later, coming at the usual time, the cousin found the shop entrance crowded. A placard hung from the counter: "Any packet 25 paise." There was such a clamour for the packets that the boy at the counter looked harried and exhausted. Old men, young men, children, beggars, and labourers, everyone fell over each other with outstretched arms, and the trays were emptied as fast as they were filled from the kitchen. By five o'clock the entire stock of sweets for the day was exhausted. Sivaraman and the other cooks came out of the kitchen, stood before Jagan, and asked, "What do we do now?"

"Go home," said Jagan. "If the sweets have been sold, our work for the day is over."

"I do not understand," said Sivaraman, turning the golden bead at his throat. "What has happened? What is all this for?"

"Let more people eat sweets, that is all; aren't they happy?"

"Do you plan to close down?" asked Sivaraman; and his assistant said, "At this rate, we will be swamped."

"It will make no difference to you," said Jagan. "We shall reduce nothing, either in quantity or quality."

"How? How can we?" asked Sivaraman.

Jagan could not easily explain what he was doing or why. The cousin sitting on the stool came to his rescue. "We are only trying some new measures to meet the competition. I will explain it all to you tomorrow." The cooks went away, and the shop emptied itself at six o'clock, the boy bringing in the bronze jug earlier than usual, saying, "Still a crowd outside waiting, sir. They are angry that they are not getting anything today."

"Tell them to come tomorrow." They could hear the shouts of the crowd outside and the captain swearing at them. "Our people must learn to be disciplined," Jagan observed.

He felt light at heart after this arrangement, but it took time for his staff to get adjusted to the idea, as they were afraid that stagnant business might limit prospects and promotions. Jagan had not thought of that, but he pretended to have taken into consideration all aspects of the question and just brushed off comments. They returned to the subject again and again. They had more time at their disposal to stand around the throne and discuss things, now that the frying operations lasted only three hours from midday and the sales only an hour. Except for the crowd at the counter vainly clamouring for more, the place became free from all activity. This was a cause of great concern for Sivaraman, who felt that the crowd might turn unruly. Jagan replied, "Be patient and watch; our people have to learn discipline and will certainly learn soon. Don't worry." To everyone in that little hall it sounded irrelevant, but they were too polite to say so.

"Maybe we shall have to prepare more," said Sivaraman, chewing a piece of tobacco in a most leisurely manner.

"No harm in trying it, but what for?" asked Jagan.

They merely mumbled, "So that no one is turned back."

"What for?" asked Jagan again. Sivaraman and his four assistants were pure technicians in the matter of confectionery; they floundered over questions of economics, marketing, and politics. Sivaraman had a sudden inspiration and answered, "Because more people are now asking for our sweets now that the price has been so much reduced."

"Oh, that is a brilliant explanation," Jagan felt, but he did not think it politic to say so; he merely remarked, "Well, that is a point of view; we will consider it after we see how it all goes for at least fifteen days." He knew that his staff viewed him as an astute businessman; although his decision was baffling, doubtless they thought he must have some sound reason for taking this step; they credited him with some canny purpose, and he could not bring himself to disillusion them. He felt curiously flattered and gratified, and, although a lover of truth generally, in this instance he enjoyed shining in a false light.

Sivaraman finally said, "Is it possible that you have found a way to draw all the business in the town to your door?"

He had just enough tact and vanity to permit himself a meaningful smile; and they felt pleased and smiled meaningfully too. He then held before them greater treasures than mere profit. He said, "You have leisure now and do not know how to use it. Let me help you. Sit down and learn how best to utilize the precious hours that come to us, not by lounging in the market-place or discussing money matters. Sit down all of you; I will read to you from the Bhagavad Gita every day for an hour. You will benefit by it. Call in the captain also if he'd like to join us." He commanded them to be seated again, looked on them with benign pity from his throne, took out his Bhagavad Gita, opened it to the first page, and began, " 'On the field of Kurukshetra two armies arrayed and ready for battle faced each other.' Do you know why they were there?"

Sivaraman, now completely relaxed, sitting crosslegged and bolt upright on the floor, said, "Of course, we all know why they were there. I am sure all these boys know too." They murmured an assent; the captain, standing respectfully apart with arms folded and his short stick under his right arm, nodded appreciatively.

Not minding what the head cook said, Jagan began again from the first line in a singsong, and felt a thrill at the sound of Sanskrit. "At this moment the great warrior Arjuna had a misgiving as to how he could fight his own uncles and cousins; his knees shook at the thought. Then God himself, who had chosen to be his charioteer, explained to him the need to fight for a cause even if you had to face your brothers, cousins, uncles, or even sons. No good has ever been achieved without a fight at the proper time. Do you understand?" All their heads nodded an assent although their minds were wandering a little; they were anxious lest he should inflict on them another repetition of the same stanza. After further explanation Jagan said, "There is no such thing as reading this book finally; it is something to be read all one's life. Mahatma Gandhi read it to us every day; was it because he did not know it or thought we did not?"

"True, true," all of them chorused.

"Mahatmaji placed his fight against Britain in the same category." The place was beginning to take on the look of a schoolroom, and that the pupils were not quite enjoying it became evident by the number of times Sivaraman got up to spit out tobacco and the others went out to blow noses or take snuff. Even the captain, the very picture of good manners, at one point pretended to notice some intruders at the door and slipped away. It was doubtful how long this could have gone on, for these men, after all, flourished in kitchen smoke and preferred frying to enlightenment; but to everyone's relief three visitors burst in. The captain strutted up, saluted and ushered the visitors before the throne as was his duty, and withdrew. The cooks lounging on the floor presented an odd spectacle at this hour when business should be at its peak and the kitchen belching fire. Jagan became incoherent and effusive when he recognized his visitors: one was the sait from Ananda Bhavan, the man who had built an enormous restaurant business within a span of fifteen years although he hailed from a province a thousand miles away; the second one ran a canteen at the law courts; the third man, who had a white beard, was a stranger. "Perhaps someone's brother," Jagan reflected. "Ah, what an honour," he kept repeating, and almost embraced them. His audience for the Bhagavad Gita melted away unobtrusively.

There were not enough seats for all the visitors, but luckily the cousin's stool was available today and Jagan fussily offered it to the bulky sait. The captain brought in an iron chair from the soda shop next door which Jagan allotted to the law-court canteen man, leaving "someone's brother" to fend for himself, and resumed his seat on the throne; it was impossible for him to occupy any other position in this hall. "Someone's brother" stood about uncertainly while they talked of politics, the weather, and general market conditions for half an hour, before coming to the point. Then the sait asked, "What is it that you have been trying to do during the last . . ."

"Four days," said the "brother."

The sait added, "He is our friend."

Jagan threw a smile at him and, encouraged, the bearded man edged nearer and sat on the platform at Jagan's feet.

The sait said, "You are making a drastic reduction in the price of your sweets?"

"Yes."

"May we know why?"

"So that more people may enjoy the eating of sweets," replied Jagan with a beatific smile.

The others looked shocked at this heresy. "What prevents more people from eating at the right price?"

"The price of the stuff itself," said Jagan, suddenly hitting upon a lucid explanation.

"It is bad business," said the canteen owner.

In answer Jagan said, "I am unhappy, my distinguished guests, that I have nothing to offer you, all our trays having become empty an hour ago."

"Then that is good business," said the sait with a twinkle in his eyes. Jagan accepted the compliment with a knowing nod, looking gratified at his own acuteness. "But why should you upset all our business?" asked the sait.

"I will ask the customers who clamour here to go to your shop, provided you promise them pure quality."

"Do you mean to say that we don't use pure stuff?"

"I don't know. I use the purest butter for frying and the best flour and spices."

"And yet you say you are able to sell a packet for twenty-five paise?" They all laughed at the joke. The sait went on, "In 1956 I used to do that myself, but now where do we get pure stuff at the right price?"

"I can help you to get the supplies if you like. As Lord Krishna says in the Gita, it is all in one's hand. You make up your mind and you will find the object of your search."

The bearded man sitting on the platform butted in to remark, "Ah, the Gita is a treasure, truly a treasure-house of wisdom."

"I never spend a moment without reading it."

"One can go on reading it all one's life," agreed the sait himself, and the canteen man said, "We all know it. The Gita also says every man must perform his duty in the right spirit and the right measure. Do you think you are doing that?" He assailed Jagan directly.

Jagan's composure was lost. He merely said, "Oh!" and covered his confusion with a simper.

Now the sait leaned forward to say with all the grimness he could muster, "If one person does it, all the others will do it also, are you aware of that?"

Jagan's mind did not take in the implications of his statement but he felt he ought to match its sharpness and answered, "What if they do?"

"Is that the line you wish to take?" asked the canteen man.

Jagan, wondering what there was so sinister in taking the line, mumbled some irrelevancy and suddenly shouted, "Captain! Get four drinks for these gentlemen from the soda shop. . . ."

There were murmurs of refusal from the assembly, but they softened towards Jagan and the sait said, "Oh no, don't take all the trouble, sir. We have come to talk serious business. Let us get through it first. Business first is my motto always."

"Otherwise how can we get on? That must be the beacon-light of conduct for all businessmen, the only philosophy," said the canteen man, and the bearded man quoted a passage from the Upanishads which proved nothing.

"What are we all talking about?" asked the sait suddenly. Jagan and the rest said nothing. The sait, who was evidently the leader of the delegation, continued, "My time is precious; at this hour I am hardly able to leave my counter, and yet I have come; does it not show the seriousness of the business that has brought us here?"

The canteen man said, "It is nearly a year since I visited this part of the city. Where can one find the time?"

"Each man is busy in his own way," said the bearded man.

"I am very glad to see you all here. We must all meet once in a way like this and discuss our problems," said Jagan, feeling that he had been left out too long.

"I am very happy that you should think so," said the sait, looking genuinely relieved. "We must all learn to live together and voice our feelings nowadays; otherwise we will be left behind in the race."

"Union is strength," said the bearded man; he attempted to illustrate his thesis with a story from the Panchatantra. "There was once upon a time . . ." he began.

This was too much for the delegation, and the sait cut him short with, "Of course, Panditji, we all know the story and its moral. As I was saying," he went on, feeling that he had the first right to speak in this assembly, "as I was saying, we have many problems. Today we are bewildered and ask ourselves why we should continue in business."

"Exactly what I have felt, but I keep it up more for the sake of my staff," said Jagan, understanding the words in the simplest terms possible.

The sait felt inspired to continue, having fallen into the groove of talking shop. "There is really no answer to our problems; people mind their own business and think that we can somehow exist and continue to exist. How they expect us to continue is more than I can understand."

"If we close our business even for a single day then they will know," said the canteen man.

"It would be actually more economical to close down our business, but we cannot do it; people will suffer; innocent office workers, labourers, and students who depend upon us for their nourishment would be the real ones to suffer," said the sait, feeling as if he were a benevolent angel conferring boons on humanity. "Our problems are numerous."

He was excessively fond of the word "problem." He mentioned the word so often that Jagan felt constrained to ask, "What problems?"

Both the sait and the canteen man turned an astonished glance at him as if they could hardly conceive of anyone in his senses asking such a question. Both of them started to talk at once, and the voices clashed and became indistinguishable as they said, "The sales tax inspectors who will not accept the accounts we render, the income-tax people who assess arbitrarily, the health inspectors, the food control which has practically driven everything underground—how are we to get the provisions for our recipes? And above all the frying medium; we can't always use pure ghee, and the government forces us to announce what we use; how can we do that when our customers like to be told, whatever they may actually consume, that they are being served pure butter-melted ghee?"

"The ideas about pure butter-melted ghee are antiquated," said the canteen man. "In fact, scientists have proved that pure butter and ghee bring on heart disease; the artificial substitutes have more vitamins."

"They are not much cheaper, either."

"Their prices are going up nearly to the level of pure ghee."

"So why not pure ghee?" asked Jagan, which really irritated his visitors. As they were mustering their wits for a repartee, the captain brought in four bottles of soda, opened the first one with an enormous plop, and held the bottle dripping, overflowing, whizzing, and hissing to the sait as the courtesy due to the leader of the delegation. The sait said with some annoyance, "I told you, I want nothing."

Jagan said, "It is only soda, lot of gas in it; take it."

Meanwhile, like a machine, the captain was popping open the other bottles and the bearded man was snatching each from his hand and passing it on; the floor became wet with the effervescence. When a bottle was offered to Jagan, he took it, but turned it ceremoniously over to the captain.

The sait said, "You wanted us to drink the soda."

"Because I know it is good," said Jagan.

"But why don't you drink it?"

"I don't drink more than four ounces of water a day," said Jagan, "and that must be boiled at night and cooled in a mud jug open to the sky. I drink no other water; even when I was in prison in those days . . ." he began, but the rest cut short his reminiscence with the question, "Have we spent this afternoon usefully?" Jagan was not sure whose responsibility it was to find an answer, but remembering that he was the host, said, "Of course; it has been an honour to receive you."

"We are happy that we understand each other now," said the sait. "I hope we can count on your cooperation."

Without thinking what they meant, Jagan said effusively, "Certainly, surely, I believe in cooperation fully."

The canteen man remarked, "If it is just some temporary policy of yours, it is not for us to question you."

"But if it's anything else," interrupted the sait, "we must all strive to maintain the tone of business; that is our common aim."

Jagan made some indistinct sounds at his throat, and they all left. He heard them drive off and prepared to wind up for the day. The captain came in to take the iron chair back to the soda shop and placed on Jagan's table a bill for the drinks. Jagan had emptied the cash collection into his drawer hours ago; he now proceeded to open it and was sorting out the various denominations when the bearded man who had gone out with the sait came back.

99

Jagan asked, "Forgotten anything?"

"No," said the man, approaching and taking his seat on the stool. "I sent them away in their car. I actually live in the next street; they gave me a lift, and I thought I might also come in with them and meet you. They were so busy talking to you, I did not like to disturb your meeting."

"I don't think I have seen you before," said Jagan.

"I live in Kabir Lane but seldom pass this way," he said, settling down on the stool for a conversational evening.

Jagan said, "I thought you were going with them."

"Why should I when my house is so near?"

"I didn't know that," said Jagan. "I don't know your name yet."

"People who knew me used to call me Chinna Dorai as distinct from my master, who was known as Peria Dorai— the small master and the big master—ah, in no way to be compared."

"Who was your master?"

"How many temples have you visited in your life?" the bearded man asked.

Today everyone seemed to be firing questions at him, but Jagan answered, "A hundred temples of all sorts, maybe more."

"The God or Gods in every one of the temples were carved by my master."

"Oh, how wonderful to know that!" said Jagan.

"The figures of Shiva the Destroyer, Vishnu the Protector, Devi, who vanquished the demon Mahisha with the dreadful weapons she bore in her eighteen arms, and the Dwarapalakas, gatekeepers at the shrine, and the designs on the doorways and the friezes on the walls, were all alike done by my master, all over the South." His eyes blazed and his beard fluttered while he spoke.

Jagan was impressed by his elocution although he did

not quite understand what he was driving at; it was at least a relief from the talk of butter and frying. His description of the Gods made Jagan regret that he had not gone near a temple for months, being wrapped up in this monotonous job of frying and cash-counting. He declared fervently, "Of course, I have visited every temple in this part of the universe, times out of count, and I know all the one hundred and eight Gods and saints enshrined along both banks of the Kaveri. I know the songs that Sambhandar composed in honour of those Gods." And he assumed a falsetto voice and sang a couple of pieces for sample.

The bearded man shut his eyes, listened, and showered praise on Jagan's musical ability and memory; which ballast of flattery he needed today because he was beginning to have misgivings about his practical wisdom. Jagan in turn expressed approval of the other's taste in music. In all this demonstration of mutual esteem the purpose of the conversation was, as usual, lost. The bearded man sang a couple of songs himself—not in a falsetto, but a full-throated voice without inhibition, and the captain at the door peeked in to make sure that things were normal within, at this busy hour, with its noise of traffic and crowds on Market Road. After the songs the bearded man returned to his main theme. "All those Gods you have seen in the temples were done by my master or his disciples."

"What was his name, did you say?"

"Don't mind what I said. We called him 'Master' and that's sufficient. There has been none other who could assume that title."

"Was he your master?"

"Yes. In his last years, he didn't like to admit anyone near him except me."

"Where did he live?"

"Not far from here. Any day you can spare a little time,

I'll take you there, It's just on the other bank of the river. You can see the trees of his garden from this side. Do you ever go across the river?"

Jagan sighed at this reminder. For years his fixed orbit had been between the statue and the shop, his mental operations being confined to Mali, the cousin, and frying. He recollected with a sigh the blaze of colours at sunset, the chatter of birds in Nallappa's Grove, and how he had often wandered along the river, lounged on the sands, or sat on the river-step with his class-fellows; how Mahatma Gandhi used to address huge assemblies on the sands of the river and how he himself, a minute speck in such a crowd, had felt his whole life change when he heard that voice. Where now were those friends, whose faces and names he could not recollect?—dead, flattened out by life, or existing in the same place under new masks like that toothless lawyer or that man who was so bent that he hardly looked up at anyone, or a dozen other familiar faces, at one time bench-companions at school and playmates around the statue every afternoon—passing each other daily but hardly uttering four syllables in twenty years?

"You have become contemplative," said the bearded man accusingly.

"Gandhi was my master," Jagan said. The bearded man showed no interest in the statement, perhaps because he was jealous of the term "master" being applied to any other claimant but his own. Eager to go back to the business on hand, he asked, "When will you find the time to go out with me?"

"Tomorrow," said Jagan promptly, and then asked, "Where? Come here at one o'clock in the afternoon. Are you going to show me your master's sculptures?"

"No, they are all in various temples, I told you. He was

regularly besieged by temple-builders. He was not the sort to keep his handiwork in his own house."

There was such intensity in his speech that Jagan apologized. "Oh, I didn't mean that. Where do you want to take me?"

"To show you the place where he lived and worked, that's all."

"Do you work there now?"

"No, I told you, I live behind this road."

"Do you make your images there?"

At this, the man burst into a big laugh and said, "Did I not tell you what I do now? I make hair-dyes. I can make the whitest hair look black. That sait is my best customer in the town. Once in four weeks I go and personally colour his hair, which otherwise would look milk-white, and he fetches me in his car, that's how I came to be with him to-day. A lucky day, because I have come to know your goodself."

"I'm also happy. I have never seen an image-maker before."

"You are not seeing one now, either. I'm only a blackener of white hair. I have come, too, to ask if you need my services. My responsibility is to make people look young. The sait appreciates my services. Ask him if you have doubts."

Jagan hesitated for the moment, and said apologetically, "I do not know if I could do it," trying to imagine the remarks of Mali and Grace. Probably Mali would not even notice; he hardly ever looked at him. Why not try at least to amuse him? He suddenly remembered that he himself was a specialist on this and allied subjects. "Diet has a lot to do with the colour of one's hair. My book on this subject will be out one day and then you will see for yourself;

if your diet is controlled according to nature's specifications, you will never see a grey hair anywhere."

"That may be the reason why the bear never has a grey hair," said the bearded man and laughed at the joke. For Jagan, though, this was a serious line of inquiry. He said solemnly, "I must consider that point when my book is finally prepared."

Chapter Eight

The pond was covered with blue lotus; the steps were mantled with moss and crumbling in. On the bank stood a small shrine supported on stone pillars, with a low roof of granite slabs blackened by weather, time, and the oven smoke of wayfarers. Over this little building loomed banyan, peepul, and mango trees, and beyond them stretched away a grove of casuarina, the wind blowing through their leaves creating a continuous murmur as of sea waves. The surroundings were covered with vegetation of every type—brambles, thorny bushes, lantana, and oleander intertwined and choked each other. The sun glittered on the pond's surface. The bearded man, who had led Jagan to this spot, remained brooding, watching some birds dive into the water.

"So quiet everywhere!" Jagan remarked, deciding to puncture the oppressive silence.

The other shook his head. "Not as it used to be. Too many buses on the highway, ever since that project in the hills . . ." His voice trailed away. "In those days," he said, "when I lived here with my master, you could not meet a soul unless you walked all the way to Nallappa's Grove and crossed into the town. In those days people did not go up the mountain as much as they do now; robbers hid themselves in the jungles, and tigers and elephants roamed the foothills." He seemed rather depressed at the thought of their giving place to highway buses.

"Why did you choose to live here?" Jagan asked.

"Where else could one live? We needed all those stones." He pointed through the thickets. "You see that nose of Mempi? For softer panel work that stone is excellent. For images of the inner sanctum, one has to cut the stone from the belly of the hill further up, though it is difficult to hew and there are more breakages than in other portions." His head seemed to throb with stony problems.

Jagan watched him in silent wonder and asked, "What would one do for food, and with one's wife and children in a place like this?"

The bearded man made a flourish as if to ward off a petty question. "My master never bothered about such things. He never married. I came to him when I was five years old. I don't know who my parents were. People used to say I was picked up by my master on the river-step."

Jagan wanted to ask, but suppressed the question, whether he might not have been born of a passing concubine to his so-called master who never married. While the bearded man remained thinking of his past, Jagan reflected, "He has the whitest beard and sells the blackest hair-dye. Why does he not apply it to his own beard?" He asked aloud, "How is your business?"—a question that he must have asked every few minutes, whenever there was a pause. The bearded man said, "Nothing to worry about, and the sales-tax people have still not come my way yet."

"That is a real blessing," said Jagan, remembering the visitations he had to endure, the inspectors and their minions rummaging his desk for day books, ledgers, and vouchers. In the end they accepted his accounts, unaware of the cash that grew from out-of-hour sales at the counter and filled the smaller jug, but he could no more help it than he could the weeds' flourishing in his back yard. He had a habitual, instinctive, and inexplicable uneasiness concerning any tax. If Gandhi had said somewhere, "Pay your sales tax uncomplainingly," he would have followed his advice, but Gandhi had made no reference to sales tax anywhere (to Jagan's knowledge).

The bearded man said, "But they are bound to wake up sooner or later, when they notice fewer grey hairs around," and chuckled.

Jagan seized this opportunity to say, "Anyway, you are an exception to your own rule."

"I like my white beard and keep it. There is no compulsion for anyone to blacken his hair. I would not have dreamt of blackening people's heads, if I had had a chance to work on stone. But you know how these things happen. My master supported me for years." ("How could he not, as you were his only son by a passing concubine?" Jagan retorted inwardly.) The bearded man pointed to a corner in the pillared hall. "He worked on those details of ornament and I had to move the block here. He lived his whole life here. All that he possessed could be contained within the palm of one's hand. I cooked a little rice for him in that corner, where you see the walls blackened. All day he sat here working on the image or we went to the quarry to hew slabs. He never saw anyone except when some temple men came to order an image. People were afraid to come here because of the snakes, but my master loved them and never approved of clearing the wild growth around. This tree was full of monkeys; you can see them now. 'I'll share the fruits of those trees with them,' he used to say. He enjoyed the company of snakes and monkeys and everything; once there was even a cheetah in the undergrowth. 'We must not monopolize this earth. They won't harm us,' he used to say, and true to his word nothing ever did. When he died one night I sat at vigil by a small oil lamp, and cremated his body beyond that pond, heaping on the dead wood and withered leaves. Next day I walked off to the city, and lived on charity here and there, until I got the idea for my business. That is all. I have nothing in my life to complain of now, but I was so well off in those days. . . ." Still brooding, he walked around the small hall, peered into an alcove. "There used to be a God in the sanctum which had been stolen years before we came here. One night my master woke me up and said, 'Let us make a new God for this temple. Then it will flourish again.' He had dreamt of a five-faced Gayatri, to be seen nowhere else, the deity of Radiance. He had even hewn the slab for it and knocked the first dents. It used to be in that yard somewhere. Let me look for it." He became suddenly active, peeped into every corner of the hall, went round to the back yard, where oleanders and hibiscus flourished and bloomed wildly. He discovered a bamboo staff amidst a clump—"Ah, this is still here!"—seized it, and strode about, looking like a statue of many thousand years' antiquity.

Watching him in this setting, it was difficult for Jagan, as he mutely followed him, to believe that he was in the twentieth century. Sweetmeat-vending, money, and his son's problems seemed remote and unrelated to him. The edge of reality itself was beginning to blur; this man from the previous milliennium seemed to be the only object worthy of notice; he looked like one possessed. He pointed to a grassy spot under a palmyra tree and said, "This is where my master's body was burnt that day. I can remember that terrible night." He stood under the palmyra with his eyes shut for a moment, muttering some holy verse. "We should

not let the body deceive us as to the true nature of our being. One is not really bone and meat. My master proved it
in his days," he declared, and as if seized with a sudden
frenzy beat down every bush with his bamboo stick,
startling a variety of creatures—lizards, chameleons, birds,
and frogs, which had lived undisturbed for years in the
green shelter. He seemed to enjoy their discomfiture and
inhaled noisily, with relish, the smell of crushed greenery.
He said, "I'm sure the cobras that live here must have quietly slipped away when we came; they are uncanny in their
habits. Very alert, very alert and watchful." Chipped-off
blocks of stone and odds and ends of sculptural pieces came
to view beneath the weeds. He pointed his staff at them,
explaining, "This was the pedestal of Vishnu, meant for
some temple; those are the arms of Saraswathi, the goddess of learning—they could not be used because of a slight
crack in the stone. My master got so upset when he noticed
the defect that he flung it out through the door and remained speechless for three days. At such moments, I used
to stay away from him, shielding myself behind the trunk
of that tamarind tree. When the mood passed he would call
me. 'But where is that other block? Where is it? The two-
foot-square one? It could not have grown limbs and walked
off—although, let me tell you, if an image is perfect, it cannot be held down on its pedestal.' I always remember the
story of the dancing figure of Nataraj, which was so perfect
that it began a cosmic dance and the town itself shook as if
an earthquake had rocked it, until a small finger on the figure was chipped off. We always do it; no one ever notices
it, but we always create a small flaw in every image; it's for
safety."

He went on talking and Jagan listened agape as if a new
world had flashed into view. He suddenly realized how narrow his whole existence had been—between the Lawley

Statue and the frying shop; Mali's antics seemed to matter naught. "Am I on the verge of a new janma?" he wondered. Nothing seemed really to matter. "Such things are common in ordinary existence and always passing," he said aloud.

The bearded man, suppressing his surprise at this sudden remark, said, "True, true, you must not lose sight of your real being, which is not mere bone and meat." He reached up to a branch of a guava tree, plucked a fruit and bit into it with the glee of a ten-year-old urchin. "This tree always gave the best fruit. Monkeys thrive on it, and during certain seasons the treetop would be as full of monkeys as leaves, you know." He pulled down the branch again, plucked off another fruit and held it for Jagan.

Jagan took it out of courtesy, but did not eat it. "I keep off sweets and salt."

"Why?" asked the other.

"Well—" how to express his whole philosophy of life in a limited jargon? He concluded, "You will find it all explained in my book." At the mention of "book" the other began to lose interest. He was used to inscriptions on stone and on palmyra leaf, and he was not enticed by the mention of the printed book. Jagan, unaffected by his attitude, added, "The printer, Nataraj, do you know him at all?" The bearded man had lost interest in the subject totally by this time. Ignoring Jagan and talking on, he failed to observe that Jagan had overcome the temptation to take a bite and had let the fruit slip to the ground, unable to decide whether it would be good or bad from the point of view of dietetics. What a shame if it was good to eat and he had surrendered it, for it was attractive, with green turning yellow on top and yellow turning red in the middle, and soft to the touch. Before he had developed his theories of sane living, he used to eat a dozen of them each day, and it might well be said that between seven and twelve years of age the aroma of guava had permanently clung to him! A huge tree had grown in their back yard, right over the tin-shed, and one day his father took an ax and cut it down, remarking, "These little devils will eat nothing else as long as this cursed tree stands. See how one by one they are going down with colic!" As Jagan followed the other about, vaguely aware of his speech, his mind was obsessed with the fruit he had abandoned, until the bearded man asked, "Are you listening to me?"

"Yes, yes, of course," Jagan said.

"We have gone round and round, but not found the slab. It must be somewhere," said the bearded man. He hugged the stick, resting his chin on it, and was lost in thought.

Jagan could not help asking, "Why are you bothered about it?"

"Very important, very important, I tell you. When I have found it, you will know." He unwrapped himself from the stick abruptly and said, "Now I remember, come with me." He moved briskly towards the pond. "Come down with me. Mind the steps—they are slippery." He went down the steps and up to his knees in water. Jagan lagged behind, unable to comprehend the other's action. "Perhaps he is going to knock me into the pond and go back to the town and report, 'The maker of sweets has vanished.'" The other's face was flushed with excitement as he looked up and cried, "Won't you come down? What if your dhoti gets wet? You can dry it later." His tone was peremptory. Jagan descended the moss-covered steps, which gave him a creepy feeling underfoot; he commented within himself: "Better meet one's fate in the hands of a sculptor." His dhoti did get wet, and he shivered slightly as he watched with fascination bees swarming on the blue lotus. He felt a sense of elevation—it would be such a wonderful moment to die, leaving the perennial problems of life to solve themselves.

While he was busy with his thought the other, who had stooped on all fours, looked up and said, "Come here," with his eyes blazing and his beard fluttering in the wind. "There is no retreat for me," thought Jagan. "He is preparing to hold my head down in the water. Should I turn back and rush away? No, not a chance of retreat," and took a further step down. He was now wet to his waist. "Cold water may be good for rheumatism, but I am not a rheumatic," he told himself. "If I do not perish in this water, I shall perish of pneumonia. In my next life, I'd like to be born . . ." His mind ran through various choices. Pet dog? Predatory cat? Street-corner donkey? Maharajah on an elephant? Anything but a money-making sweet-maker with a spoilt son.

The bearded man, still on all fours, now commanded, "Plunge your hand in here and feel . . ."

Jagan obeyed, precariously poising himself on the slippery surface.

"What do you feel there?" the other asked imperiously.

Jagan noted that ever since they had stepped into this garden, the man had become more and more authoritarian. He was no longer the tame hair-blackener on Kabir Street but a sort of leader of the forces, a petty chieftain used to having his orders carried out without question. Nothing like implicit obedience. Jagan plunged his arms into the water, and shuddered when something clamped its jaws on his hands. "Oh!" he screamed. It was only the other's hand-grip. Now a smile appeared on the bearded face as he propelled Jagan's hand through the water over a stone surface. "This is the stone I meant. Let us take it out. Hold it at your end properly. Can't you lift it? I am not surprised. If you ate normally like other human beings, or at least consumed some of the sweets that you sell, you would be in better shape. I remember my master put this stone into the water because it needed the water treatment to bring out its surface grains. Do you feel the notches, the first ones he made? He had started to work on it but suddenly decided that it needed water-seasoning; he always said that the longer a stone stayed in water . . ." He looked about in despair. "If you could only make up your mind to lift it, it is only will power you lack. This is not after all a big statue but a small one, hardly a couple of feet—when it is fully worked it will hardly be eighteen inches. Can't you lift a stone that is going to be just eighteen inches high? I am surprised. I only want you to give me a hand, not lift it yourself. Help me."

He was so cajoling and bullying by turns that finally Jagan began to feel that he ought to exert himself. He girt himself for the task by tying his upper cloth around his head and tucking up his dhoti in a businesslike manner. He held his breath, gripped his end of the block, pausing for a moment to consider whether at his age he was well advised to carry a slab of stone up wet steps. But this was no time to consult one's own inclinations or welfare. When they reached the top of the steps, he just let go the stone, threw his entire length flat on the grass, and shut his eyes.

When Jagan revived, he found the other rolling the stone over and explaining, "This would be the top; come closer and you will see the lines marked by my master with the bodkin, the outline of the Goddess." He scraped the moss off the stone, which was drying in patches, and stood lost in contemplation. To Jagan's eyes it was no different from any other block of stone; even the scratches originally made by the master were hardly convincing; but the bearded man seemed to feel intoxicated at the sight of it. "This is where the Goddess's hands come; she is ten-armed, and except for the one which indicates protection and the one offering a blessing, all the other arms hold a variety of divine articles." For some time he was lost in visions of the Goddess and then began to narrate a story.

"I know the story of the Goddess," said Jagan.

"Who doesn't?" replied the hair-blackener. "But still it's always good to hear it over and over again; you will always have the protection of Devi, and everything you attempt will turn out successful." And he broke into a loud Sanskrit song. The birds in the trees fluttered at the sudden outbreak of noise. Frogs at the edge of the pond sprang back into the water, and Jagan's gaze was held by the delicate tracks on the surface left by aquatic creatures invisibly coursing.

"If I can devote my life to the completion of this task I will die in peace," said the other.

"How old are you?" asked Jagan.

"Do you want to know? Then guess."

Such speculation always embarrassed Jagan. He could never be sure whether people asking that question liked to look younger or older than their years. In either case, he felt he could not be drawn into a debate, and so said, "I can't say . . ." observing the man's head, which was bald. ("No place for his dye there," he thought.)

"I am sixty-nine," said the other abruptly in a matter-of-fact manner. "I'm prepared to die peacefully on my seventieth birthday, if I can finish that image and install it on its pedestal."

"Will you be able to complete it in a year?" Jagan asked.

"I may or may not," said the other. "How can I say? It's in God's hands. With all that water-seasoning, the slab may suddenly split in the middle, and then what does one do?" Several possibilities occurred to Jagan. While he was fumbling for an answer, the other declared: "Bury the broken image and start anew with fresh quarrying and a fresh seasoning in water, that's all."

"Suppose the second one breaks," Jagan asked.

"That'd be an inauspicious thought and question," said the other grimly and added, "The second stone does not generally crack." They sat in silence. The other said, "Ten hands! Oh, the very picture thrills me." He burst into another song in Sanskrit, "*Mukta-vidruma-hema* . . ." When he had completed it he asked: "Do you understand the meaning of that?"

"Yes, in a way," replied Jagan cautiously.

"It only means the Goddess whose countenance has the radiance of *mukta*, that is pearl, and *hema*, that is gold, and then the blue of the sapphire or the sky, and then the redness of the coral. . . ." He took a deep breath, paused, and continued, "Since she is the light that illumines the Sun himself, she combines in her all colours and every kind of radiance, symbolized by five heads of different colours. She possesses ten hands, each holding a different object: a conch, which is the origin of sound, a discus, which gives the universe its motion, a goad to suppress evil forces, a rope that causes bonds, lotus flowers for beauty and symmetry, and a *kapalam*, a begging bowl made of a bleached human skull. She combines in her divinity everything we perceive and feel, from the bare, dry bone to all beauty in creation. . . ."

Jagan was filled with awe and reverence at the picture that arose in his mind. The bearded man sat brooding for a while, then said, "My master always meditated on this form and wanted to create the image for others to contemplate. That was his aim and if I can carry it out, I'll abandon all other work in life." He came down to business. "It's only a man like you that can help me."

Jagan gave a start on hearing this. He had never thought that the task would concern him. "How? How?" he asked anxiously, and before the other could collect his thoughts, added, "Don't think too much of me. No, no, after all, I'm a humble merchant."

The other said, "Why don't you buy this garden and install the Goddess?"

"I . . . I . . . do not know," replied Jagan, thickening his armour of self-defence, and tried to laugh the question off, but the other became deadly earnest, half rose, and, waving a finger close to Jagan's eyes, said, "Very well, I understand. I only thought it would do you good to have a retreat like this."

"Yes, yes, God knows I need a retreat. You know, my friend, at some stage in one's life one must uproot oneself from the accustomed surroundings and disappear so that others may continue in peace."

"It would be the most accredited procedure according to our scriptures—husband and wife must vanish into the forest at some stage in their lives, leaving the affairs of the world to younger people."

Jagan felt so heartily in agreement that he wanted to explain why he needed an escape—his wife's death, son's growth and strange later development, and how his ancient home behind the Lawley Statue was beginning to resemble hell on earth—but he held his tongue. He felt shy and reserved about talking of his son—like one not wishing to exhibit his sores.

Chapter Nine

Jagan now had a separate key with which he let himself into his house softly. He crossed the passage, and shut the door between his part of the house and his son's. Then he hooked his upper cloth on a nail in the wall, stripped off his jibba, passed on to the back yard, poured a lot of cold water over himself, and came out of the bathroom. Feeling hungry today, he set a bowl of water on the kitchen oven, cut up a few vegetables, and threw them in, along with a small measure of coarsely ground wheat. The day had been hot, and he preferred to remain without a vest. While his dinner was cooking, he stood before the Gods for a second with eyes shut, then lit an oil wick and took out his small charka from behind a large bureau, inserted a hank of cotton, turned the wheel, and drew a fine thread out, watching its growth with a sensuous pleasure: the slight whirring noise of the wheel and the thread growing out of it between one's thumb and forefinger were very comforting, stilling the nerves and thoughts. Gandhi had prescribed spinning for the economic ills of the country, but also for any deep agitation of the mind.

Jagan's mind was in a turmoil; at the same time he had a

feeling that his identity was undergoing a change. If that was so, why should he bother or resist the idea? Committed to various things until yesterday, to the shop and the family, he was a different man at this moment. An internal transformation had taken place; although he still cared for the shop and house, this latest contact had affected him profoundly. The Gods must have taken pity on his isolated, floundering condition and sent this white-bearded saviour. As he turned the spinning wheel, sitting there in the courtyard, with the sky-reaching coconut trees of the neighbourhood waving amidst the stars, his mind analysed everything with the utmost clarity. He wondered if the bearded man might not be a visitation from another planet—otherwise, why did he come to his shop exactly when he needed him? Who really needed help and from whom? The man had said that he needed help for installing the image of the Goddess, while he himself thought that he was being helped. He could not solve the puzzle easily, and so left it alone. Anyway, it was a reposeful memory: the man had really communicated a thrilling vision when he described the Goddess with five heads. Should he help him or not to complete his task? He knew nothing about him. How could he trust him? On what basis? After he finished the image, what then? Live in his company in that wilderness and encourage him to carve more images? What would happen to the hair-dye? Perhaps he'd be expected to take charge of the business and run it in addition to his sweets. Run after white hair on a large scale, earn more money, and ruin Mali further? He suspended his reflections and his spinning for a moment in order to go up and inspect the vegetables on the stove; then came back to his wheel, thinking of the fixed law of nature by which wheat was cooked in exactly thirty minutes; if it was cooked for forty minutes, it became gruel and was no good nutritionally; in food, food-making and food-eating, what was important was precision. It was a science—that's what he was trying to establish in his book, which should have been in the hands of the public but for Nataraj. Why was Nataraj indifferent to this task, while he had printed the prospectus for Mali with alacrity? Perhaps he didn't like his ideas; but a printer did not have to like an idea in order to print it. He should rather be like Sivaraman, who had to fry something even if he didn't care for it himself.

The cotton got thinner and longer as if it were the soft dough from which Sivaraman sometimes drew fine vermicelli strands; the wheel groaned and purred and cleared its throat. Through the open roof he could see the crescent moon passing behind the coconut trees, a couple of wispy white clouds racing across its face. Perhaps the monsoon will be breaking earlier this year, he reflected. One enters a new life at the appointed time and it's foolish to resist this fact. He was no longer the father of Mali, the maker of sweets and gatherer of money each day; he was gradually, unnoticed, becoming something else, perhaps a supporter of the bearded sculptor—or was he really his ward?

There was a knock on the door, which was lost in the purring of the spinning wheel. The middle door opened and Mali came in, looking like an arrival from another planet in the dim light (Jagan had fitted only ten-watt bulbs in the light sockets in order to benefit the human retina). Excited at the sight of his son, Jagan quickly snatched a towel and hid his chest under it; if he had known that he was coming, he'd have had his jibba on. He left his spinning and leaped up to fetch a stool to seat Mali. Mali took it from his hand, muttering, "What a fuss you make!", planted it in the open court, and sat on it, while Jagan stood about uncertainly.

"Sit down, father," Mali commanded, "but don't turn that wheel; it's noisy and I want to talk to you."

At this Jagan felt a sinking at his stomach and smacked his drying lips. He moved away from his spinning wheel, folded his arms across his chest, and asked, "Now, tell me, what do you want?"

"Everyone talks about you in the town," said Mali in a tone of accusation.

Jagan slightly stiffened but said nothing. The sinking in the pit of his stomach gradually left him as he remembered that one ought not to resist when circumstances pushed one across the threshold of a new personality. "What do they talk about?" he asked. He was beginning to shed the awe in which he had held his son. "Who are 'they'?"

"The Ananda Bhavan sait and a number of others were discussing you yesterday."

Jagan did not wish to pursue the subject and so mumbled, "Let them." He felt unhappy at having to speak in a new tone of voice to Mali, from whom he used to pine for a word: "I am a new personality and have to speak a new tongue." He could not judge the expression on his son's face because the crescent moon was now completely gone and his bulb enveloped everything in a pale yellow light, making all faces and all moods look alike.

Mali took a paper from his pocket, tried to read it, and said petulantly, "Why can't you have brighter light?"

Jagan replied, "Light rays should soothe the optic nerves and not stimulate them."

The boy smiled cynically. "This cable came in the afternoon from my associates."

When he heard the word "associates," Jagan did not need to hear anything more. He was not scared, as he would have been forty-eight hours ago. "In a few hours, I have undergone a lot of changes, but the boy doesn't know it," he reflected. "Let me be kind to him. No harm in showing him kindness. After all . . ." He felt a stab of habitual tenderness, and regret at sounding so officious to Mali. "What does the cable say?"

Mali spread it out again to catch the light, failed, and repeated from memory, "Please cable . . . status our project."

Jagan looked bewildered. This was not the English he knew. Except for the word "cable," the rest did not mean anything. He said, "Why should they ask you to cable? An ordinary letter will do."

The boy said, "We have to move pretty fast in business matters. Why can't you leave that to me? I know what to do. What shall I say in reply?"

"What is 'status'? Whose status are they talking about?"

Mali clenched his fists and said, "Are we going through with our manufacturing business or are we not?"

"Do you propose to talk about it now?" asked Jagan.

"I must know about it."

Jagan felt a sudden pity for the boy sitting there forlorn and puzzled, and he cursed the barrier which seemed to raise itself whenever they came together. He pleaded, "Son, I'll leave you in charge of the shop, it's yours. Take it."

The boy made a wry face at the mention of the shop; fortunately the dim light did not reveal it fully. "I tell you once for all, I don't want to be . . ." He merely concluded, "I have learnt valuable things in the United States at a cost of several thousand dollars. Why can't our country make use of my knowledge? And I . . . I can't . . ." Although he avoided the phrase "vendor of sweets," his repugnance for the occupation came out unmistakably. They remained silent, and Mali added the final touch. "In any case your business is worth nothing now."

"Who told you that?"

"Everyone in the trade is talking about you. What are you trying to do, anyway?"

Jagan remained silent. Mali again described his fiction-writing machine in detail, and repeated the contents of his prospectus. Jagan listened while the stars ran their course. When Mali paused, having reached the end of his prospectus, Jagan just asked, "Where is Grace?"

"Why?" asked the son.

Jagan had no answer; and he was not bound to answer every question.

Mali insisted, "I have to know whether you are coming into our business or not."

"What'll you do if I say no?"

"Grace will have to go back; we will have to buy her an air ticket, that's all."

"What has it to do with her?" asked Jagan; the connections were baffling, like the wiring at the back of the radio panel.

"Why would she stay here?" asked the boy plainly. "She has nothing to do."

"I do not understand what you are talking about. I have never been able to understand you at all. Call her, let me talk to her." He had got used to the presence of Grace in the house, and he felt desolate at the thought of losing her.

"She has gone out," said Mali briefly.

"Where, at this time of the night?"

"She can go where she pleases. Why should anyone question her?"

"No, it's not that," said Jagan. Fate seemed to decree that there should be no communication between them. Some invisible force twisted their tongues when they wanted to speak and made them say the wrong things. Jagan stood up desperately, bent down close to his son's face, and cried,

"Where does she go? Why does she go? Is she unhappy here?"

Mali rose to his feet and said, "Who are you to stop her from going where she pleases? She is a free person, not like the daughters-in-law in our miserable country."

Jagan said, "I just want to know why she is thinking of going, that's all. She is, of course, free. Who says she is not? Has anything made her unhappy?"

"What is there to keep her happy?" cried Mali. "This is a miserable place with no life in it. She was used to a good life. She came here to work, and she is going back because she has no work to do."

Jagan swallowed back the words he wanted to blurt out: "But she is sweeping and cleaning the house. This is a big house and she has enough work to keep her engaged for the whole day. What more does she want?"

Mali announced, "She came here for the project, to work with me; didn't you see her name in the notice?"

Jagan had learnt the art of ignoring questions. Mali got up, saying, "If she has nothing to do here, she goes back, that's all. Her air ticket must be bought immediately."

"But a wife must be with her husband, whatever happens."

"That was in your day," said Mali, and left the room.

Jagan lost his sleep that night. The obscurity of the whole business worried him. Grace was out of sight. He liked her presence in the house, which filled a serious lacuna. Where had Mali hidden her at the moment? He wouldn't even admit that he knew where she had gone. Was this how a man kept track of his wife?

Chapter Ten

He had to wait for his chance to meet Grace. He knew by the sound of the duster in the front part of the house that she was back, but would she come as usual to his rooms and attend to things? No. It was over ten days since she had come near him. She seemed to be avoiding him. He felt depressed at the thought. What had he done that she should avoid him? Had she shown all that considerateness only in order that he might invest in their story machine? Now that he had made his position clear, the barrier between him and the other two was growing more impregnable than ever, and there was absolutely no way of his approaching her and asking for an explanation. He wondered if he could go in and talk to her, but what would be the use? With Mali there, how could he ask her for verification? It would be at best a formal greeting and nothing more. Though he was ready to leave for his shop, he sat on his cot vaguely hoping either that Grace would come his way, or that Mali would go out on one of his errands and he could have a word with her. But there was no sign of either happening. Mali went on typing in his room; after a while the sound of sweeping ceased, and he could hear some exchange of words between the two; then even that ceased, and a tre-

mendous stillness reigned over the house. There seemed
to be no hope. He quietly slipped out of the house and
reached his shop, where life went on as usual, only the
clamour at the counter destroying the peace of the afternoon. Of late, Jagan had been unable to concentrate on the
Bhagavad Gita until the crowd had dispersed. They be-
haved as if they were entitled to their sweets irrespective
of whether there was stock or not, which made Jagan doubt
if he had been wise in reducing the price and whether he
should not go back to the original prices.

The cousin had been absent for several days. He explained, "I had to be away in the Tirupathi Hills with the
judge's family; they had taken two of their grandchildren
to the temple for their first shave. It was a grand trip; they
had engaged three cottages and the whole temple was open
to them—an influential man. They would not listen when
I told them that I could not afford to keep away so long;
they nearly abducted me."

"You are wanted everywhere," said Jagan. "I have
wanted you badly."

"I am at your service."

"Has the reduction in prices affected the quality of our
sweets?"

"Such a thing is unthinkable, I tell you."

"The Ananda Bhavan sait was here. . . ."

"I know, I know," said the cousin. "They are talking
about you all the time!"

"What do they say?" Jagan got suddenly interested in
the market reactions.

"It seems you have agreed to resume your prices soon."

"I don't know. . . . I don't think I have said any such
thing," said Jagan.

The cousin said, "At least that is what they think. It will
do them good to stand in the line and see how you

do things. I wouldn't be at all surprised if their men are in the crowd and buy the sweets cheap here and sell them at their own price in their shops." It hadn't occurred to Jagan that this was a possibility. He looked desperate when he heard it, and the cousin had to say, "I was only joking; don't let it worry you."

Jagan asked, "Have you been seeing Mali recently?"

"He was at the judge's house last evening. His son is his friend. He called me aside. He is ever so fond of me, calls me his uncle. Nothing changes him. . . ."

Jagan sighed, "Why does he not talk to me properly? He can't speak two sentences without upsetting me."

The cousin, pleased at the superior position he was enjoying, said rather patronizingly, "Don't let it upset you. You are a wise man and you must not think of these things too much."

"What did he tell you?"

"He called me into the garden while his friend had gone in to wash and told me that Grace was going back to America soon. Did you hear that?"

"Yes, yes, but I did not understand why."

The cousin said, "She is going on business. That's what he told me. Something to do with his machine. You see how plucky these girls are! She goes thousands of miles to settle business matters, while we do not even understand what they are doing!"

Jagan did not correct him but kept his knowledge of facts to himself. "Well, of course, I had heard that, but I wanted to know if there was anything more."

"His business seems to be promising," said the cousin. "The Ananda Bhavan sait and a few others have promised to buy shares in his company."

Jagan asked with genuine wonderment, "How does he talk to them?"

"He is all over the town and very active. I meet him here, there, and everywhere."

"I want your help," said Jagan. "Don't laugh at me. I have to speak to Grace and find out a few things for myself." He explained the situation in a roundabout way without letting the cousin know too much.

The cousin knew that a lot of things were being hidden from him, but he did not mind. He said, "I see Grace sometimes visiting Dr. Kuruvilla's house. She has a friend there whom she knew in America. Shall I speak to her and say that you want to see her?"

"Won't Mali be with her?"

"Sometimes she spends her time with the girls in that house, while Mali goes out with his friends."

Jagan had to hold his soul in peace for the next two days, while the cousin thought out ways of decoying Mali, leaving the line clear for Jagan to speak to Grace. One afternoon he arrived on his usual tasting duty. Wiping his mouth with his towel, he said, "If you are prepared to leave the shop, you can meet Grace at home. Mali is waiting for me at the judge's house. I have promised to go with him to look for a plot of ground on the Hill Road."

"What for?"

"For building his factory."

"What rubbish! He is talking like a big financier! If he has the money for it, why does he ask me?"

"Everyone in the town thinks of him as a big businessman. He talks well!"

"Yes, to everyone except me," said Jagan resentfully.

The cousin said, "We'll talk of all that later. Will you go home? This is the right moment. Mali is going out of town and won't be back until evening. I'll stay here until you come back. There will be others to go with Mali."

Jagan went home, washed himself, went into the puja room, stood before the Gods, and prayed, "Please help me, enlighten me. I don't know what to do and how to do it." He stood in meditation for a second, then, reinforced in spirit, knocked on the middle door in the hall. It was unusual for him to come home at this hour; and the place looked strangely different, with the afternoon sun coming in at odd corners through the open court. "This looks like somebody else's home," he reflected, and it confirmed again his recent feeling that he was no longer his old self. He recollected the bearded man's advice during their rambles: "At first don't hurry, but when you decide, be swift and positive." That was more or less what he had learnt from Gandhi, but the lesson seemed to have worn out. He remembered how as a volunteer over twenty years ago he had rushed into the British Collector's bungalow and climbed the roof in order to bring down the Union Jack and plant the Indian flag in its place. Helmeted police were standing guard in the compound, but the speed of his action completely took them by surprise and they had to clamber after him to the roof, but not before he had seized the Union Jack in a crocodile grip and hugged the flag-post while attempting to plant his own flag. They had to beat him and crack open his skull in order to make him let go his hold. He opened his eyes fifteen days later in the hospital, and lay forgotten in a prison afterwards. "There are times when a Satyagrahi has to act first and think afterwards," his leaders had advised. Once a Satyagrahi, always a Satyagrahi. If one was not acting for truth against the British, one was acting for truth in some other matter, in personal affairs, in all sorts of things. His training was always there, but somehow had dimmed inexplicably. With all these reflections, he reinforced his ego before venturing to knock on the door of Mali's apartment.

Grace opened the door and exclaimed, "Father! You here at this hour! How unusual!"

Jagan went straight to the point. "I have to talk to you. Will you come here or should I go in there?"

"Please come in. Come to the hall. The chairs there are comfortable."

He followed her and took his seat on the sofa. She sat in her chair, one finger twirling a chain around her neck. She had a book open on a side table. She was wearing a yellow kimono and looked very much like a Japanese. "She looks different each day!" he thought, and suppressing his impulse to ask, "Are you sure you are not a Japanese today?" said aloud, "What are you reading?"

"Nothing very important," and she mentioned some title.

"Go straight to the point," he told himself. "You have beaten about the bush and practically lost contact with your son; don't lose your daughter too." His first question was "I don't see you in my house nowadays. Why?"

She went red in the face. Her lips twitched and she remained silent. Observing her discomfiture, he said, "Don't bother to answer my question." He left her a little time to recover her composure, then asked, "Do you wish to go back to your country?"

Once again her lips twitched, her face went red, and she cast her longish eyes down and remained silent. A crow cawed, perched on the tiles of the open courtyard. Its raucous note broke the awful silence. She muttered, "Ah, that crow has come! Excuse me." She bustled about, went into her kitchen, came out with a piece of bread in her hand, and tossed it on the roof; the crow picked it up and flew off. Presently more crows came and sat on the roof and cawed. "This is the worst of it. They all clamour, but I don't really have enough for all of them," she said.

Jagan could not help saying, "The same thing is happening to me in my shop. The whole town clamours for my sweets, but really the sales close before four in the afternoon."

She received this in silence. Jagan felt nervous. All the resolutions he had made vanished without a trace. He was scared of Grace. He felt she might break down if he asked any more questions. He sensed a deep-seated disturbance in her and became anxious to leave her alone, whatever the mystery might be. When a clock struck four he got up, saying with extraordinary clarity, "I must be back at the shop."

She walked to the door with him silently. When he passed her, she said in a matter-of-fact way, "Father, Mo wants me to go back."

"Why?" Jagan asked, halting.

She hesitated. Jagan feared she might cry, but she said very calmly, "It's all over, that's all."

"What's over?" She didn't answer. He asked, "Is it his idea or yours?"

She repeated, "He wants me to go back. He says he can't afford to keep me here any more." These new facets of Mali now revealed were startling, and Jagan found himself tongue-tied. She went on. "I used to work. I had two thousand dollars when I came here. All that's gone."

"How?"

She merely said, "Mo has no more use for me."

"Use or no use, my wife—well, you know, I looked after her all her life."

Grace said rather shyly, "The only good part of it is, there is no child."

He found some portions of her talk obscure but could not ask explicitly for explanations. He said, "If you read our puranas, you will find that the wife's place is beside her husband whatever may happen."

"But we are not married," Grace said simply. "He promised he'd marry me in the Indian way, because I liked it, and brought me here."

"And the marriage didn't take place, after coming here?"

"Wouldn't you have known it if it had?" she said.

It was too much to swallow and digest at one sitting. Jagan wailed, "I don't know what to make of it all."

"Will you come back for a while and take a seat? I'll explain. I feel awkward standing here," Grace said.

He stood looking at the girl. She looked so good and virtuous; he had relied on her so much, and yet here she was living in sin and talking casually about it all. What breed of creatures were these? he wondered. They had tainted his ancient home. He had borne much from them. He said coldly, "No, I'm not coming in now. Let me go back to the shop."

When the cousin came at 4:30 p.m. Jagan shouted, "Come here, I am waiting for you." The cousin held up his arm as much as to say, "Wait till I finish my savouring duties." While he was in the kitchen, Jagan's ardour cooled. He had mentally rehearsed a speech beginning, "Do you know . . ." but actually asked when the cousin emerged from the kitchen, "How well do you know Mali?"

The cousin spent a little time gazing at the tailor across the road pedalling his sewing machine, which, as Jagan knew, was a sign that the cousin was in deep thought. He shook him out of it by saying, "Mali is not married."

The cousin suppressed many questions that arose in his mind, wondered if he was expected to attempt some new matchmaking for Mali, and began, "Of course, if you give the word, people are ready to snatch his horoscope; even the judge was mentioning that he had a brother's niecein-law who was anxious for a match with your family. . . ."

Jagan felt slightly elevated by this news but suddenly remembered that he was not fated to live an ordinary peaceful life. . . . "Captain, those school children!"

The captain, not knowing whether he was expected to shoo them off or give them gifts, cried back, "What shall I do with them, sir?"

"Send them away. If you show some consideration once, they expect it forever and ever; our people have no self-respect."

"I know you want to reduce the price of all the stuff further, but cannot," said the cousin.

"No sense in upsetting the social balance. I don't wish to make enemies of that Ananda Bhavan sait or the others. There are all sorts of persons at their back."

The cousin agreed in order to dispose of the question then and there, and let the other go on with the more interesting subject of Mali. He egged him on. "Did you meet the girl today?"

"Why do you say 'the girl' instead of Mali's wife?" Jagan asked with a certain amount of vicious pleasure.

The cousin, for the first time feeling trapped by this question, said generally, "She seems to be a good girl. When I met her yesterday at—"

Before he could finish his sentence Jagan said, "I am not doubting her goodness, but I repeat that she is not married to Mali at all." The cousin received the statement in silence, fearing that anything he said might smack of scandal. Jagan went on. "She told me so herself; why should I doubt her?"

The cousin said simply, "Then why not let her go back to her country as Mali wants?" This sounded such a rational approach to the crisis that Jagan had nothing further to say for a long while. It was very difficult to recollect what he had meant to say or to refresh his memory with the righteous indignation that he had felt. The cousin added, "Our young men live in a different world from ours and we must not let ourselves be upset too much by certain things they do."

This sounded a sagelike statement, but Jagan could not accept the theory of indifference which the cousin, still not knowing the exact facts, was developing. Jagan said, "This sort of thing is unheard of in our family. Even my grandfather's brother, who was known to be immoral, never did this sort of thing. When he was not married he never claimed that he was married, although . . ."

"I have heard my father speak about him. He was certainly married to three wives and had numerous other women. He never shirked a responsibility." They were deriving a vicarious pleasure from going into the details of lechery practised by their forefathers.

"I can't understand how two young persons can live together like this without being married," said Jagan. He let his mind revel in sensuous imaginings of what had gone on within the walls of his house. "I feel my home is tainted now. I find it difficult to go back there."

The cousin said, "You have heard only one side of the story. Why not speak to Mali and find out the other?"

"He has already told me he wants her to go."

"It is because his business is not developing," said the cousin.

"What business!" cried Jagan so emphatically that the cook carrying a tray to the front stall stood arrested and nearly dropped it from his hand, at which Jagan glared at him and said, "You get on with your job. I am not speaking to you." He added in a whisper, "These boys are not what they used to be; they are becoming awfully inquisitive. I am sure he knows all about this affair."

The cousin now brought the matter down to a practical level, as he always did. "Why do you let this affect you so much? It is, after all, their business."

"But I feel it is my home that is being dirtied. Mali is my son. Grace is not my daughter-in-law."

"Oh, that is a very wrong, selfish view to take," said the cousin, feeling his way now, and getting the measure of Jagan's mental needs. His role was to help Jagan crystallize his attitudes in a crisis. He added, "What is all your study of the Gita worth if you cannot keep your mind untouched by all this? You yourself have explained to me that one should not identify oneself with objects or circumstances."

Jagan accepted this compliment with great pleasure, although if he had questioned it, he might not have been able to explain exactly what he had said, or why or when. Obliged to admit his devotion to the Gita and the wisdom derived from it, he mumbled, "We are blinded by our attachments. Every attachment creates a delusion and we are carried away by it. . . ."

"Too true, too true," said the cousin. "Equanimity is more important than anything else in life."

"That is what I am seeking but never attain!" Jagan wailed, and quietened his thoughts for a moment. Suddenly he remembered that he had been fooled by the young people and that the house which had remained unsullied for generations had this new taint to carry. How could he live in the same house with them? He was on the point of saying, "I have half a mind to tell them to go where they please and do what they like, but not in my house. . . ." But he checked himself; it was a statement that his tongue refused to phrase. Certain things acquired an evil complexion if phrased, but remained harmless in the mind. "How do you expect me to go on living there?"

"If you have the back-door entrance, use it and don't go near their portions. Where else could they go now?"

"That is true, housing conditions being what they are. Moreover, people will talk." He begged, "Please don't let anyone know."

The cousin threw up his arms in horror. "Unthinkable. What you say to me is a sacred trust, believe me."

Assured by this protestation, Jagan said, "What shall I do now?"

"About what?"

"About Mali and that girl."

The cousin gave a clear-headed statement. "Get through their marriage very quickly in the hill temple. It can be arranged within a few hours."

"Alas, I don't know what her caste is; so how can I?"

"Oh, she can be converted. I know some persons who will do it."

A burden was removed from his shoulders. Jagan said, "You are my saviour, I don't know where I should be without you."

Chapter Eleven

Jagan barricaded himself in completely. He derived a peculiar excitement in performing all the actions of a purificatory nature. He shut the communicating door between his part of the dwelling and Mali's and locked it on his side. He did everything possible to insulate himself from the evil radiations of an unmarried couple living together. There was a ventilator between the two portions of the house; he dragged up an old stool, and with the help of a long bamboo shut it tight. Now the isolation, more an insulation, was complete. He gave up the use of the front door, as it took him through a common passage trodden by the feet of the tainters. A whole morning he kept himself busy with these arrangements, dragging the stool hither and thither and shifting the ladder. After locking the back door of his house when he left for his shop, he took a side lane which led to the main street. He noted that this path was overgrown with thorns and weeds. "I must take out my spade and clear it," he said to himself. Nearly fifty years had elapsed since he had traversed this lane. In those days, when his father's family had lived in a hut in the back yard and the front portion was growing up little by little, he and his brother used to hunt for grasshoppers amidst the weeds. All the blazing afternoons they would be active in this pursuit while the Malgudi summer scorched everything, and even the grasshoppers were reluctant to leave the paltry shade of the weed-plants. His elder brother carried a small tin; he cupped his palm over the grasshopper and trapped it, and, if it was a large one, transferred it to his tin as befitting an elder brother; if it was a little one, it was passed on to Jagan; but on no account would Jagan be permitted to catch one himself. He could only stand behind his brother and wait for his luck, with his own little tin in hand. This would go on all afternoon, until the grasshoppers learnt to anticipate their footfalls and hop off to safety. Sometimes their sister would track them down here, and follow them doggedly, uttering sinister remarks. "You are killing the animals here. I'll tell Father; they are found dead every day in the tins. You will both go to hell." Jagan, afraid of this blackmailer, would plead with her to leave them alone, but his elder brother would say, "Let her talk. No one wants her here. If she speaks to Father, I'll wring her neck," and rear himself up menacingly, and she would run away screaming in terror. "They never liked me," reflected Jagan. The sister married a wealthy village idiot, became a rustic, and brought forth an ugly brood of children, and that brother cut all contact after the division of their father's estate. Ah, how intrigued they would be if only they knew the full story of Mali! Since the advent of Grace, all his relations had ostracized him. The only reminder he had had from his sister was a postcard a year ago on the back of which she had written, "We are ashamed to refer to you as a brother. Even when you joined Gandhi and lost all sense of caste, dining and rubbing shoulders with untouchables, going to jail and getting up to all kinds of shameful things, we didn't mind. But now is it a fact that you have a beef-eating Christian girl for a daughter-in-law? I can hardly call you a brother in the presence of my in-laws. No one can blame Mali, with a father like you. . . ." And she had concluded with the gratifying thought that their parents were fortunately dead and spared the indignity of watching these unsavoury activities. Jagan had heard that his brother, who lived in Vinayak Street, often spoke of him in anger and shame; and he never invited him to join him in performing the anniversary ceremonies for their father. He was an orthodox man who managed the headquarters of a religious order established ten centuries ago, with a million followers, and he had begun to disapprove of Jagan's outlook long ago. His remarks were brought to Jagan from time to time by common friends and relatives and occasionally by the cousin, whose standing was secure everywhere. The elder brother had once remarked, "How can you expect a good type of son when you have a father like Jagan?" What would they say if they knew the latest development? They would doubtless remove themselves further. Jagan felt grateful for being an outcast, for it absolved him from obligations as a member of the family. Otherwise they would be making constant demands on his time and energy, compelling him to spend all his time in family conclaves, sitting on carpets with a lot of kinsmen exchanging banalities while awaiting the call for the ceremonial feast. Thus he had escaped the marriages of his nieces, the birthdays of his brother's successive children, and several funerals.

Jagan was passing the statue when the green car with Mali and Grace drove past him. Mali applied the brake and waited for Jagan to come up. Grace opened the car door and asked, "Want a lift anywhere?"

"No," said Jagan and tried to pass on.

"Were you spring-cleaning your home, Father? I heard the sounds of your activity."

"Yes, I was trying to clean my surroundings," Jagan said, putting into the words a new meaning. Mali sat staring ahead saying nothing. Jagan noted the serious careworn look in his eyes and felt a tug at heart. If he could have recklessly announced, "Long live your story-writing machine! Here, take my bank-book, it's yours. I have no use for it," all problems would be at an end. No, not all the problems. Marriage? These two sitting so close with their legs touching and not married! What was their relationship now? Now they were saying things against each other although they were nestling so close!

Later Jagan confided in the cousin, "I had half a mind to accost them then and there, but I let them go. I will find another opportunity to clear up this whole business once and for all."

By his architectural arrangements Jagan had isolated himself so thoroughly that he didn't notice until a fortnight later that Grace was no longer there, and that there had been hardly any movement in the front part of the house. One morning he was so intrigued by the silence that he stood beside his door and applied his eyes to the keyhole, after removing a little paper ball he had plugged into it. He saw no one, but he heard some movement in another room. He put the plug back into the keyhole, straightened himself, went round by the back yard and arrived at the front window, and stood peering through the half-curtain. He couldn't see anything, but Mali called from within, "Who is it?" Jagan tried to tiptoe away. A little later, Mali opened his window, saying, "You could have knocked."

"No, no," said Jagan, "I didn't want to . . ." He tried to

retrace his steps through the side lane. Mali watched him for a moment, then cried, "Father!" Jagan was thrilled. After many days he was called "Father" again. He stopped.

The boy asked, "Why do you prowl around like this?"

Jagan said in confusion, "Where is Grace?"

"Why do you want her?" Mali asked gruffly.

"Because I have not seen her for a long time," said Jagan, feeling bold enough to make that statement.

Mali said, "How can you hope to see anyone when you have sealed yourself off and use the back door? It looks silly."

Jagan pretended to attend to a jasmine bush as he noticed his neighbour watching them with great interest. "Ever since he bought that house, this man has done nothing except watch our house. I wish I had bought it when it was offered. I could have given it to Mali. He'd have been near enough and far enough too." Jagan was lost in these speculations for a moment, and Mali, also noticing the neighbour, suppressed his conversation. Jagan said, "I want to talk to you both; why don't you come out?"

Mali withdrew his head from the window and came out by the front door. He wore a fancy dressing gown, and had stuck his feet into slippers. He seemed to cower back and re-coil from the bright Indian sunlight. It was as if he was unique and could not come out except with a fanfare and appropriate pageantry. He approached his father and said, "I don't like that guy over there watching us. Don't talk loudly."

"All right," Jagan whispered hoarsely. The effort to sup-press his natural tone to a whisper choked him and puffed up the veins on his neck. He was unused to secrecies.

Mali said, "Why should we talk in the garden? Can't we go in?"

Jagan was afraid to mention the actual reason, and slurred over it by saying, "I thought it was pleasant here."

"Yes," said Mali cynically, "with the sun scorching and all the neighbours providing the audience."

The sting was lost on Jagan, whose only delight was that he had today caught his son in a talking mood. "Let us move on to the shade in that corner. The man won't see us there."

"But all the passers-by will watch us," said Mali.

Jagan asked, "Why should not people look at us? What's wrong with us?"

"People must respect other people's privacy, that's all. We don't find it in this country. In America no one stares at others."

"If we avoided each other's looks, how should we understand each other? What is one ashamed of, that one's face must be hidden?" Mali could not carry on this debate. He found his father in an extraordinarily controversial mood today. He gave up his point. Jagan, triumphant, asked, "Is Grace inside or not? I'd like to talk to you both on a matter of importance."

"She is not here. She has gone to stay with some friends for a few days."

"When did she go?" Jagan felt that his son was likely to resent his questioning tone, so he expanded the theme: "I was wondering if it was not a very long time since I saw her."

"You have sealed off the middle door and use the back door. What's your idea, Father?" While Jagan was choosing words for a plausible answer, the boy went on. "Do you think my business is going to be dropped because you have shut the door? Our correspondence goes on and I must know where we stand. Do you imagine you have made me drop the project?"

It was a pity that they should be rushing to the edge of the precipice as usual. Jagan tried to give another turn to their talks. "You must both be married soon."

"What are you trying to say?" screamed Mali. Jagan explained. Mali merely said, "You have been listening to nonsense. I never knew you could listen to such gossip."

Jagan noted with pleasure that the boy refrained from calling him "silly" again. He asked, "Does Grace gossip about herself? Anyway, I do not want to go into all that again. There is a very small temple, where you can go through a quick marriage. No one need be invited, just the three of us and a priest, and you can be done with the whole business in an hour."

"Grace has been getting funny notions, that's why I told you to pack her off, but you grudged the expenditure," said Mali. "She is not in her right mind; she must go to a psychiatrist."

"What's that?"

"Don't you know what a psychiatrist is? What a back-wood this is, where nothing is known." With that Mali turned and went in, leaving Jagan transfixed to the spot. He tried to recollect the words that Mali had said and tried to make out their meaning. There was no meaning. What was a psychiatrist? What would he do? Before he could sort it out in his mind, the neighbour edged along to the fence, commenting, "So rare to see you! What is your son doing?"

"He is in business with some American businessmen."

"Oh, that's very good. So he will earn dollars for our country. Very good, very good . . ." On this pleasant note Jagan tore himself away, because he felt that the next question was going to be about the daughter-in-law. Funny situation!—not knowing whether she is a daughter-in-law or not. He was totally at a loss to decide who was lying.

Chapter Twelve

Jagan was worried. The entire day passed with his mind completely obsessed. He was functioning with only a part of himself. Sivaraman's inquiries, the coming in of cash, and the arrival and departure of his cousin at the appointed hour were all mechanically gone through. His cousin ate, spoke of various things, and waited as usual to talk of Mali, but Jagan was in no mood to encourage him, and the cousin gave up with resignation. "Sometimes he talks, sometimes he doesn't. Take him as he comes, that's all," he thought and slipped away at the right moment.

Jagan counted the cash and made the entries, but his mind worked on only one theme only, the puzzle created by Mali. At every encounter he displayed a new facet, which might or might not have any relevance to the previous one. Jagan was reminded of the concept of *Viswarupa*, that he read about in the Bhagavad Gita. When the warrior Arjuna hesitated to perform his duty on the battlefield, God came to him in the guise of his charioteer and then revealed Himself in all His immensity. On one side He was thousand-faced. "I behold You, infinite in forms on all sides, with countless arms, stomachs, mouths, and eyes; neither Your end nor middle nor beginning do I see . . ." quoted Jagan in-

wardly, at the same time remaining rational enough to realize the irreverence of the comparison.

That evening Jagan sat all alone on the pedestal of the
statue. All the others who had congregated around it were
gone. Sir Frederick thrust his top into the world of sparkling stars. The night was hot; the still air and heat were suf-
focating. He saw his house beyond the statue; unless he
went and switched on a light, there would be no light in it.
It stood up, sinister, dark, and silent. There was a time when
it seethed with life, lamps burning in every room, and
during the festivals hundreds of mud lamps would be lit and
arrayed all along the parapet. Theirs had been the brightest
home in those days. That was long before the birth of Mali,
years even before his marriage. He suddenly recollected
the exact point in time when he had shed his bachelorhood.
That day when he had travelled to the village of Kuppam
in order to take a look at the bride proposed for him by the
elders of his family. They had to go by train to Myel, a tiny
red-tiled railway station set amidst emerald-green rice fields,
two stations beyond Trichy. From Myel he had to go on in
a cart drawn by a pair of bullocks over a bumpy mud track,
and in some places even over cultivated fields. The future
bride's younger brother, who had come to meet him as a
piece of courtesy, was also in the carriage. Jagan was in a
happy mood and laughed uncontrollably at the way they
were progressing in the cross-country run. Every time the
wheels sank into a sandy patch and the cartman got down and
heaved them out with oaths, Jagan felt tickled; but the boy
stuck to his seat and remained grim and silent. He had been
trained to show respect to a brother-in-law by being reserved; that boy had the grimmest face in the country. Ultimately he grew a long moustache as a commissioned air-

force officer, and was lost sight of in the Burma Campaign of 1942.

Jagan's father had sent his elder son to accompany him and commanded Jagan, "Don't stare at the girl. I have seen her and I know she is good-looking. Don't imagine you are a big judge of persons." At the end of the bumpy journey, he was received with a lot of fuss and seated on a carpet spread on the pyol of an ancient house. His future father-in-law and a number of his relations had assembled to have a look at the proposed bridegroom and measure him up from different angles. They all engaged him in conversation and tried to judge of his intelligence and outlook. Jagan had already been warned by his elder brother not to be too communicative, as a certain mysteriousness was invaluable in a son-in-law. Everyone kept asking as if in a chorus, "How was your journey?" Jagan stroked his tuft with one hand, fumbled with the rim of his cap and threw furtive glances at his brother for a signal, and when his brother nodded slightly, he answered, "Oh, yes, it was good."

"Did you have comfortable seats in the train?" asked one examiner sitting at the farthest corner of the pyol; and this time Jagan said on his own, "Of course." It was a matter of propriety to say a good word about the journey when the railway ran over their territory. "What is your subject of study at the college?" asked another one, and Jagan answered, "History," without waiting for his brother's sanction. (Later, when they were alone, his brother nudged him and said, "You should have said 'mathematics,' because I know those people would prefer a mathematical son-in-law; all the boys in this part of the country are first-rate mathematicians." To make matters worse, Jagan had not only said, "History," but had also attempted some humorous explanations about his capacity in mathematics.) While talking,

Jagan cast furtive glances into the hall in the hope of catching a glimpse of his future bride. He had as yet no idea what she would look like. At home he had been shown a rather overtouched shiny photograph of her mounted within a floral border: a sharp-faced young person with tightly braided hair. The photographer had managed to achieve his task without revealing what the girl's eyes looked like, and Jagan, when presented with the photograph, had been unable to scrutinize it for long, because his father was watching him. He was racked with a doubt whether the girl might not be squint-eyed, since it was well known that photographers tried to slur over such facts for purposes of marriage. He liked her height as she stood with her elbow resting on a corner stand with a flower vase on it; her fingers looked slender and long. She had been decorated with so many ornaments that it was impossible to guess what she really looked like, and of course the photographer had imparted the appropriate complexion.

Now Jagan was going to clear all his doubts; engaged in answering the questions of the assembly, he was seriously wondering when the call would come for him to enter the house and examine his bride. They brought a silver tray heaped with golden-hued jilebi and bonda made of raw banana, and coffee brown and hot, in two silver tumblers, at the sight of which Jagan became hungrier than ever. Left to himself he would have gobbled up the entire lot (his food theories had not yet begun), but a glance from his brother restrained him. The protocol was inflexible: they were honoured visitors, on whose verdict would depend the future of the girl; it was a highly serious and important role, and they were expected to carry themselves with dignity without displaying any emotion even at the sight of jilebi; even if one was maddeningly hungry one had to say, "Oh, why all this? I cannot eat. We have just had coffee and everything in the train. . . ." Jagan mumbled this sentence with the utmost reluctance, jointly with his brother, who uttered it with great clarity. All the same, the code demanded that their hosts should press the delicacies upon them. Then one would have to break off the jilebi minutely with the tip of one's fingers and transfer it to one's mouth, and generally display reluctance or even aversion until pressed again, and then just to please others eat two or three bits in succession and then take an elegant sip of coffee. The essence of behaviour in these circumstances consisted in seeming to do things for the sake of one's hosts. One left half a cup of coffee undrunk and the edibles practically untouched; one peeled a banana indifferently, broke off a couple of inches, and ate it without moving a muscle, leaving the rest of the fruit to be thrown away. This was Jagan's first occasion for displaying ceremonial behaviour. At home he was well known for his gluttony; indeed his mother admired him for it. When he came home from school he always rummaged in the kitchen cupboard and stuffed his mouth with cashew nuts, coconut, jaggery, and varied fried edibles which his mother prepared for his benefit. On Saturdays and Sundays, when he stayed at home, he ate nonstop, and this always elicited the utmost appreciation from his father, who would remark, "This son of ours must have been a rat in his last life, considering his nibbling capacity." For one with such a reputation it was rather hard to observe the restraints of protocol; his fingers itched, his palate was agitated. However, after tasting a minute portion of the repast, Jagan resolutely pushed away the tray. Then his future mother-in-law appeared at the doorway, unobtrusively studied the features of her son-in-law, and announced with all gentleness, "Why not adjourn inside?" —addressing no one in particular. Whereupon the master of the house rose to his feet saying, "Why don't you all come in?" which was again a kind of code. Although everyone was fully aware of the purpose of the young man's visit, one had to view the main purpose casually, neither side displaying too much interest or anxiety. Everyone sitting on the pyol got up. Jagan's brother, a born diplomat, was the last but one to respond, and the last was Jagan, though he was burning with impatience. He was worried, too, lest he should perpetrate some silly *faux pas* and become a disgrace to his family, whose previous experience in such matters was none too happy. Jagan had become an eligible bachelor three years before and had inspected four would-be brides so far. On two occasions he had kept staring at the girls in open-mouthed wonder because they happened to be stunningly ugly; on another occasion he undisguisedly watched the legs of the girl as she walked in because she had been reputed to be lame. For these lapses he had been severely reprimanded, and his action went into the repertory of family jokes. Whenever his maternal uncles or others from his mother's side arrived, and gathered after dinner in the courtyard looking for scapegoats for their gossip, invariably Jagan supplied the text. This time, they had tried to prevent mistakes by sending his elder brother to chaperone him through this delicate mission. The brother was certainly not going to spare the authority vested in him; he was literally keeping his eye on him, commanding and manipulating him by narrowing his eyelids or opening them wide.

Next they were all led to the central hall of the village home. In honour of this visit many cluttering benches, rolls of bedding, and other odds and ends had been moved to a corner and covered with a huge carpet. On the floor was spread an enormous striped carpet; incense sticks were lit so as to overwhelm the smell of the cowshed at the back yard. "These fellows from the city are fussy and don't know how to live with domestic animals," her father had said, or so Jagan's wife reported later in life. For Jagan the scene was heavenly; he felt a momentary satisfaction at the thought that all these preparations were for his sake (even if it was the brother who was the controller). They showed him a seat and the rest arranged themselves around. Jagan kept thinking, "With so many around my view is going to be obstructed and then no one should blame me if I demand a second appearance." There could be no such thing as a second appearance, but his imagination was running wild. Some voices approached, and Jagan stiffened and resolutely avoided his brother's glance. A harmonium sounded mysteriously somewhere inside; to the accompaniment of its discordant notes a slightly masculine voice (he was to become familiar with it, later in life) sang Thyagaraja's "Telisi Rama Chintana . . ." [The powers of the very thought of Rama]. "Ambika is singing with the harmonium; she felt too shy to sing in the presence of so many, so she is singing in the room. She can sing very well. I have got her a teacher from the town." The father mentioned a place six miles away. Jagan was certainly not in a critical enough mood to say they should have spared themselves the trouble. The music ceased. There were stirrings inside, some arguments and protests, and then a little girl with tightly plaited hair emerged grinning with the comment, "Ambika refuses to come out, she feels shy," at which all the elders joked and laughed. The master of the house raised his voice and called, "Ambika, come on, come on, there's nothing to be afraid of in these days." And he addressed the women inside in a general way, "Don't make fun of her, she will be all right. . . ." After this preamble a tall girl emerged swishing her lace sari, facing the assembly and smiling, and Jagan's heart gave a thump. "Not at all like the photo, so tall! I can't believe . . ." The master of the house saved further specu-

lation by announcing, "She is my first daughter," and the
tall girl said, "Ambika is coming." The rest Jagan did not
hear; he lost interest in the tall girl who was only a sort of
advance guard for her younger sister, who came with
downcast eyes and bowed head and moved across the arena
so fast that Jagan could not take in any detail. "Not short
nor tall, nor fat nor puny . . ." Jagan could not arrange
her in any clear outline. The details overlapped, but producing only impressions of an agreeable nature, and not
provoking aversion as on the previous occasions. "How is
she to know what I look like if she flits by so fast?" Jagan
speculated. "I don't care what my brother is going to say
later; for the present I am going to stare, gaze, and study. I
don't care what anybody thinks." He stared unwinkingly
at the girl. She had a thick wad of wavy hair, plaited and
decorated with flowers, and many pieces of jewellery spar-
kled on her person. She wore a light green sari which suited
her complexion. Was she fair or dusky? Who could say?
His vision was clouded with a happy haze, and he might
keep peering at her a whole day with none to disturb his
study, yet he could never clear his doubts about her personality. During these muddled moments, she shot one
lightning glance at him, which somehow, through the fates,
coincided with a look he was himself shooting at her, and
their eyes met, and Jagan's heart palpitated and raced; and
before he could do anything about it, it was all over. The
assembly was on its feet, people were leaving, and the vision
was gone.

All through their journey back, Jagan remained pensive.
His brother did not try to disturb his mood. Their train was
due to arrive two hours later, but the double-bullock cart
had put them down at the little railway station before sunset and had returned to the village. Jagan sat on a weighing

platform, looking away at a range of mountains beyond the green fields. His brother, who was pacing up and down impatiently, stopped by for a minute to say, "Why should they have brought and dumped us down here so early?"

Jagan merely said, "They have their own reasons, I suppose. I heard the young fellow say that the bullocks had some difficulty at night. . . ."

"Ah, you are already assuming the role of their spokesman? Does that mean . . . ?"

Jagan nodded an assent somewhat shyly and stood up and asked eagerly, "How will they know? Should we not tell them?"

His brother stood stiff and said, "I hope you have not been a fool, telling anyone that you like the girl. One doesn't cheapen oneself."

"No, no," protested Jagan. "I was with you all the time and never spoke to anyone except to say good-bye to them generally." When he had to leave his feet had tarried and moved at snail's pace in the hope that the girl would peep out of the doorway, at least to prove that she loved him as conveyed by her lightning look; he wanted somehow to assure her that he would marry her and that he was not in the least prejudiced by her harmonium music; in his excited state of mind it seemed to him a matter of the utmost urgency to convey to her this message, and also if she really cared for him she should show some slight sign at the parting. He had never expected that such factors as train-times and the poor sight of bullocks would tear him away from his beloved's aura so unceremoniously.

On the train journey he remained brooding. He was troubled by the feeling that he had missed the chance, somehow, to say farewell to his beloved; the thought of her was extremely comforting, soothing, and also in a quiet way thrilling. His brother, now having no policing to do, was asleep in his seat, leaving Jagan free to go back to the village in his thoughts and roam unfettered. Thinking it over, Jagan felt charmed by every bit of the expedition: their house was nice and cosy, their hall smelt beautifully of incense which somehow blended successfully with the cow-dung smell from their cattleshed; the harmonium was out of tune, but it would not be proper to judge of her music from it. Her voice was gruff because she had had to adjust it to that horrid instrument; he was sure that she really had a sweet voice to suit her face. Then he too fell asleep during the rest of the journey. They had to get off and change into another train at some junction, and they arrived at Malgudi station early in the morning. His brother hailed a jutka and haggled with the man, and they started out for their ancient home at Lawley Extension. Milkmen were out with their cows, a few cyclists were on the move to reach the single textile mill of the town by the time its doors should open. Except for these the city was still asleep.

When the brothers arrived home, their mother was sprinkling water on the front doorstep and decorating it with flour. While his brother was still arguing with the jutka man, who was demanding two annas more than the agreed fare, Jagan picked up his little bag and passed into the house. His mother just smiled at him and asked no questions. His father was drawing water from the well in the back yard; he glanced at Jagan and went on with his work. His sister was circumambulating the sacred tulasi plant in the central yard and grinned at him mischievously, while her lips were muttering prayers. Jagan retired to his room asking himself, "Is no one interested in my opinion of the girl? No one is prepared to inquire whether I like her or not. Does it mean that they are all opposed to the idea?" Nor did his brother pause to enlighten anyone, but proceeded to the back yard in order to help his father at the well.

But somehow the information leaked out and his sister was the first to come to his room when he was about to leave for the college, her eyes glittering with mischief. "Aye! Hai!" she cried and clicked her tongue provocatively. "Someone is getting married soon. . . ." The house was in great excitement. His brother's wife had been summoned from a holiday at her parents' house in order to help with the arrangements for the wedding. Stage by stage the tempo increased. His father wrote numerous postcards every day between noon and three and carried them to the railway station in order to make sure that they went by the mail train. He had many relatives whom he highly respected, elders without whose sanction he never proceeded in any matter. Every day the postman's arrival was awaited by him at ten o'clock. In those days a postcard cost only three pies, but one could cram on its face and back as many hundred words as one pleased. After receiving the approvals from his elders, Jagan's father carried on several consultations with his wife in whispers in a far-off corner of the second courtyard. Jagan, as became a junior, was careful not to show too much personal interest in his marriage, but he was anxious to know what was going on. He would have been snubbed if he had inquired. He had to depend upon his younger sister, who stood about casually while the elders talked, eavesdropped, and brought him news. She would seek him out as he sat at his desk apparently studying, and then whisper to him, "Granduncle has approved." "Father is writing to the bride's people tomorrow; they are waiting for an auspicious time." "Father wants a dowry of five thousand rupees," which really worried Jagan. Suppose the other refused? Then what? "They want to have the marriage celebrated in September." Only three months! Jagan felt scared at the thought of becoming a married man in three months. It was all right as long as one dreamed of a girl and theoretically speculated about marriage, but to become a positive and concrete husband—it was a terrifying reality. "Why do they want to have the marriage so soon?" he asked.

Father's letter of approval went to Kuppam village. Many, many letters passed between the parties. A voluminous correspondence grew, which Jagan's father harpooned methodically onto a long iron spike with a circular wooden stop at one end, by which system they had preserved their family correspondence from time immemorial. One evening the bride's party arrived with huge brass trays covered with betel leaves, fruits, saffron, new clothes, a silver bowl of fragrant sandal paste, a huge heap of sugar crystals on a silver plate, and a pair of silver lamps. A dozen priests were assembled in the hall. A few neighbours and relatives had been invited and Jagan was given a new dhoti and made to sit in the centre of the assembly. They then unfolded a sheet of paper, on which they had previously spent a considerable time drafting the exact wedding notice, getting the names down correctly. The senior priest of the house, a gaunt old man, stood up and read the notice aloud, his voice quivering with nervousness. It announced that Jagannath, son of so-and-so, was to marry Ambika, daughter of so-and-so, on the tenth of September, etc., etc. The father of the bride handed this important document ceremoniously to Jagan's father, together with an envelope in which he had put currency notes, half the dowry in advance, and gently suggested, "Please ask your elder son to count the cash." Jagan's father made some deprecating sounds but passed the envelope on to his elder son for counting, who lost no time in performing the task and confirming, "Two thousand five hundred."

"It was not necessary to count," said Jagan's father gracefully, "but since you insisted on it . . ."

"In money matters it is best to be assured. How could I be

THE VENDOR OF SWEETS

sure that my counting was perfect? I always like to get cash counted again and again," said Jagan's father-in-law, at which everyone laughed as if it were a brilliant piece of humour. Then they all adjourned for a grand feast prepared by a company of expert cooks. Huge plantain leaves were spread out in the second court, with silver tumblers and bowls for each guest and a dozen delicacies and side dishes in addition to heaps of softly cooked ivory-like rice. A pipe-and-drum party seated in the front part of the house created enough din to make it known to the whole town that a marriage was being settled. The house had been brilliantly lit with numerous brass lamps as well as gas lamps, which shed an enormous amount of greenish illumination everywhere. Jagan felt overwhelmed by the celebrations. He kept thinking, "All this for my marriage! How seriously they have taken it; no backing out now." By the midnight train the bride's party were seen off. When they were gone, Jagan's mother and her relations went in and lost no time in assessing the value of the clothes and silver left by them as presents. They were satisfied with the weight and design of the silverware. Mother expressed her utmost approval by telling Jagan, "Your father-in-law is not a mean sort, see how solid all the presents are!" Jagan, identifying himself with that family, felt personally complimented.

The house wore an appearance of extraordinary activity as September approached. Jagan lost count of time. His end-of-term examinations were over, and his father had permitted him to take time off from college and assist the people at home. His mother went about saying, "Although we are the bridegroom party, we cannot spare ourselves; there are things to do." Clothes had to be chosen for the bride and others, for which purpose Mother and her relations went to the Universal Saree Emporium and spent eight hours at a stretch examining gold borders, fabric, and hundreds of saris. Jagan spent much time at his tailor's shop measuring himself for silk shirts and a dark suit; somehow his mother and the others seemed keen that the bridegroom should appear in a dark suit during the wedding procession. Jagan would have preferred to be clad in his dhoti and jibba at all times, but he was forced by everyone to accept a tweed suit. His elder brother was very vehement on the subject, having himself gone through it all some years ago. He also took charge of the printing of invitation cards and ran between Truth Printing and their home and prepared an elaborate list of addresses. Father harassed everyone about the list, asking if so-and-so had been included, and if not, to do it at once. He woke them up at midnight to suggest a name just occurring to him. He did not want any friend or relation remotely connected with Jagan to be overlooked. No one had ever suspected that Father would be such a consummate sender-out of invitations or could collect or recollect so many names, although he was never sure whether the name or initials were correct (sometimes he knew a person only by a pet name), whether so-and-so was living at that address, or even whether he was alive at all.

They sent out three thousand invitations. The result was that an enormous crowd turned up by every bus, train, and vehicle at the wedding in Kuppam village. Jagan's whole time was spent in greeting the guests or prostrating himself at their feet if they were older relatives. The priests compelled him to sit before the holy fire performing complicated rites and reciting sacred mantras; his consolation was that during most of these he had to be clasping his wife's hand; he felt enormously responsible as he glanced at the sacred thali he had knotted around her neck at the most auspicious moment of the ceremonies. He was overwhelmed by the scent of flowers and jasmine garlands and holy smoke, the feel of expensive silks and lace on his person, and the crackling new saris in which his wife appeared from time to time draped as in a vision. Her voice was not so gruff as it had sounded in the company of the harmonium; she had an enchanting smile, voice, and laugh, and she spoke to him with shy reserve whenever he was able to corner her and snatch a little privacy in the house, which was crowded every inch with guests and visitors. He found the company of so many a bother and distraction. Whenever he found a moment to talk to his wife someone or other would butt in with the remark, "Come on, come on, enough, don't get attached to the apron strings yet; you have a whole life to sit and admire your wife, whereas you will lose sight of us after the marriage." These were routine jokes and interruptions in any marriage party, but Jagan felt particularly martyred and would have been happier with fewer relatives and friends around. The noise, the music of drums and pipes, the jokes and feasting went on for three days and ended with a photographer organizing a huge group photo with the bride and the bridegroom seated in the centre. The celebrations, on the whole, concluded peacefully, although at one stage a certain bitterness arose over the quality of the coffee supplied to the bridegroom's house by their hosts, and one of Jagan's uncles, a very elderly man, threatened to leave the marriage party.

There was one other embarrassment on the night of the wedding feast. Someone who held the highest precedence in the family hierarchy (Jagan's father's cousin, a seventy-five-year-old man who had come all the way from Berhampore for the marriage) was given a half-torn banana leaf to dine on and was seated in the company of children instead of in the top row. This threatened to develop into a first-class crisis, but the girl's father openly apologized for the slip and all was forgotten. Something that upset all the womenfolk of the bridegroom's party was that the bride was not provided with the gold waist-belt that had been promised when the original list of jewellery was drawn up. When the piece was finally delivered, it was found to be made not of one gold sheet but of a number of little gold bars intertwined with silk cords. The women felt that this was downright cheating. "They are saving the gold!" they commented angrily. They would have even gone to the extent of stopping the marriage but for the fact that Jagan did not approve of all this hullabaloo over a gold belt, explaining to his mother, "This is the latest fashion; nowadays the girls do not want to be weighed down with all that massive gold." At which they became very critical of him, saying that he had already become hen-pecked, and was already an unpaid advocate for his wife's family. Even his brother managed to take him aside during this crisis and say, "Don't make a fool of yourself so soon. Why don't you leave these problems for womenfolk to discuss in the way they want?" Jagan had the temerity to reply, "It is because they are criticizing my wife, poor girl!" At this demonstration of loyalty his brother left him with a wry smile, saying, "You are obsessed, it is no use talking to you."

Jagan was given a room in the middle block. When he and his wife shut the door, they were in a world of their own within the confines of the heavy four posters. At the performance of the consummation ceremony, Jagan's father had insisted on the nuptial suite being furnished properly at the expense of the bride's party. In one corner of the room Jagan was supposed to have his study (he still had his examinations to face). When they were alone, Jagan spent all his time in love-making. He lost count of time. He found his education a big nuisance, cut his classes, and came back home and sneaked into his room and failed in every examination, forcing his father to comment that Ambika should be sent back to her parents' house for at least six months if Jagan was ever to take his degree. At home Jagan spent very little time with his sister, mother, or brother, as he used to, but shut himself in and awaited his wife's arrival. But she had her share of duties in a large joint household. It would be unseemly for a daughter-in-law to seek her husband's company when the others were busy in the house in various ways. Ambika often enough reminded Jagan of her obligations as a daughter-in-law, but he was blind to everything except his own inclinations. When he came home and waited in his room for his wife's company and she was busy elsewhere, he sulked and quarrelled with her or pretended to be absorbed in his studies when she came. His wife always liked to have him in a pleasant mood and sooner or later would yield to his inordinate demands. His father severely reprimanded him when he found him indifferent to his studies. His mother often commented, "A son is a son until the wife comes," feeling bitter that he could spare so little time for the others at home. His younger sister said, "Who may you be, stranger? We have forgotten your face." And his wife herself often said, "Please don't create all this embarrassment for me. At least pretend that you are interested in the others." His elder brother took him into the garden and advised, "I know how you feel about things. I have passed through it all myself. If you spend four hours in your bedroom, at least give the others an hour now and then; otherwise you make yourself unpopular at home." With one thing and another Jagan's stock was pretty low at home, but he did not care, as he lived in a perfect intoxication of husbandhood. Later, when his wife failed to have a baby and there were whispers and rumours, Jagan told his wife, "I wish people could see us now on this side of the door, and then they would stop talking. . . ."

Despite all his bragging there was no outside proof of his manhood. They had been married almost ten years now; he had failed repeatedly in the Intermediate and was now failing in the B.A. class, and still there was no sign of a child in the house. His brother had moved off to Vinayak Street with his entire family, which had become quite a crowd now. His sister was married and had gone to her husband's house. The big house had become silent, and people began to notice how empty it was. Jagan's mother began to grumble that there were no children at home; it was one more stick to beat the daughter-in-law with. When she was tired with housework, such as washing and scrubbing the floor of the entire house, she went about muttering, "All one asks of a girl is that she at least bring some children into a house as a normal person should; no one is asking for gold and silver; one may get cheated with regard to a gold belt even. Why can't a girl bear children as a million others in the world do?" All this was heard by the daughter-in-law scrubbing another part of the floor; she went on with her work without replying and took it out of Jagan when the door shut on them for the night. Sometimes she treated it as a joke as they sat, he with his B.A. text before him and she on the edge of the table with her legs swinging. "I dread the monthly periods nowadays. . . . They will start commenting. . . ."

"Why don't you pretend as some modern girls do that you are not in the month?" But that was a frivolous suggestion. In an orthodox household with all the pujas and the Gods, a menstruating woman had to isolate herself, as the emanations from her person were supposed to create a sort of magnetic defilement, and for three days she was fed in a far-off corner of the house and was unable to move about freely. Jagan was very irritated and cried, "Are they not satiated with children? My brother has provided enough children for several houses and my sister has begun in the true tradition with three children in four years. Why can't they be satisfied with the state of affairs as they are now?"

"Because your mother would have nothing to comment on if we had a child?" Ambika suggested, then mumbled, "As far as our family is concerned, all my sisters have many children, and your mother's insinuation that I am infertile . . ."

Jagan at once rushed into a defence of his own family. "On our side too there can be no misgiving. Do you know there is a group photo of my grandmother at the centre with all her children and grandchildren, and you do know how many heads you can count?"

"Forty? Fifty?" asked Ambika. "We have a group photo in our house with our grandmother; do you know how many children and grandchildren and great-grandchildren there are?"

"One hundred and twenty?" asked Jagan mischievously.

His wife replied, "No, don't try to joke about it; one hundred and three; and the photographer, it seems, charged four times his usual price." She was reddening under her skin; her temper was slightly rising as she said, "We are not an impotent family."

Jagan was irked by her suggestion and looked up from his book with consternation. He had no answer to give. His devotion to bed had unconsciously diminished lately. Thinking it over, he recollected how often he rolled up a carpet, took a pillow, and went out to sleep on the veranda, grumbling about the heat. "It is getting to be very hot here; shall I sleep on the veranda? Would you be afraid?"

"Afraid of what?" Ambika would ask, jokingly at first,

but gradually, as time went by, with irritation. He hardly noticed her mood and went out and slept. This had become a more or less permanent arrangement except when she returned, after a long absence, from her father's house, when he would give her passionate attention for a week running, hardly worrying about whether he was adequate; it was a question that he never at any time asked himself or his wife. He felt fatigued by all the apparatus of sex, its promises and its futility, the sadness and the sweat at the end of it all, and he assumed that his wife shared his outlook. Moreover, he had read in a book that Nature had never meant sex to be anything more than a means of propagation of the species, that one drop of white blood was equal to forty drops of red blood, and that seminal waste and nervous exhaustion reduced one's longevity, the essence of all achievement being celibacy and conservation.

It had became imperative for him to produce a child, and he didn't know what more he could do about it. Ambika herself was beginning to crave for one. He had to do something about it. She sulked and blamed him with her looks. When she saw him rolling up his carpet, she said rather bitterly, "Why don't you go and sleep at the foot of Lawley Statue? It must be much cooler there." When she taunted him thus, he felt extremely confused and attempted to joke it off with, "That statue was not built for us to sleep on," which even as he was uttering it sounded extremely silly in his own ears. When she taunted him further, he would put out the light, and pull her to the bed, and roll about, imagining himself to be the Sheik in the Hollywood film in which Rudolph Valentino demonstrated the art of ravishing women.

His father suddenly said one morning, "Next Tuesday we are going to the temple on Badri Hill. You had better apply for two days' leave from your college. Your wife will also come." When Father said anything so specific there could be no discussion of the subject. Jagan was about to leave for his college. His father, who generally spent his time in the back garden, had come up to the middle part of the house to tell him this, which itself indicated the seriousness of the situation. Still, Jagan had the hardihood to ask, "Why are we going to that temple?"

His father said, "The temple is known as Santana Krishna; a visit to it is the only known remedy for barrenness in women."

Jagan blushed and wanted to assure his father of his wife's fecundity and described to him the group photo in their house with her grandmother and the one hundred and three others, but he felt tongue-tied; one didn't discuss these things with one's father—nor with one's mother. He was a determined student this year, having made up his mind to pass his B.A. in order to prove that husbandhood was quite compatible with scholarship; that would at least prevent people from blaming his wife for his failure. Whenever the results came out and he had failed, there were pointed references within Ambika's hearing, so that the moment the bedroom door shut she would say, "Why don't you pick up your books and go away to a hostel? Your mother seems to think I am always lying on your lap, preventing you from touching your books."

She looked so outraged that he felt like mitigating the seriousness with a joke of his own brand: "If I have been failing it is because I don't believe this education is important, that is all."

"Your mother remarked that, being uneducated myself, I want to drag you down to my own level."

"Why don't you put your fingers into your ears whenever Mother talks in that strain?"

163

"Why don't you use your intelligence and pass your examination?"

He said, "Yes, that is also a good idea," and applied himself to the task with all his might. He never arrived late for his class, never missed a lesson, and drew up a general chart of subjects and a working timetable. He sat at his desk and studied far into the night. Into this nicely readjusted life his father came crashing with his plan for visiting the temple.

Jagan pleaded, "Can't we go after the examinations?"

His father glared at him and said, "We have waited long enough," and then, feeling that he sounded too commanding, added, "This is the only month when we can go up the hill; if the rains start we shan't be able to get there. Full of leeches and such things. Ten months in the year it is raining up there."

The base of the hill had to be reached by bus. The party consisted of Jagan and his wife, his father and mother. He felt touched by his father's solicitude in offering to climb the hill at his age. His mother looked extraordinarily pleased at reaching a solution at last for the barrenness of her daughter-in-law. She went on saying, "All good things only come with time. Otherwise, why would I not have thought of all this earlier, last year for instance?" She was bawling over the noise of the bus as they occupied a long seat, clutching their little bundles. Ambika felt a little shy. Some other woman in the bus asked across the aisle, "Where are you going?"

"To the temple on Badri Hill."

"Ah, the right time to go, and you will be blessed with children."

"Not me," said Jagan's mother. "I have enough." And they all laughed.

A man sitting beside the woman leaned forward to say,

"If the God blesses you, you may have twins. I know from experience!" And they all laughed again.

"One does not ask for twins; they are difficult to tend. We once had twins in the house of a distant relative, and the parents just went mad, both the babies demanding feed at the same moment or rejecting it at the same moment. I shall be happy if my daughter-in-law has a child, the next following in the normal way," said Jagan's mother.

"How many sons have you?" asked the woman, and they went into details of their family arrangements and setup. Someone on the back seat was sick and the bus had to be stopped every now and then for him to lean out and relieve himself. Ambika, as became the daughter-in-law of the house, sat beside Jagan's mother, and Jagan sat beside his father, who had the businesslike aspect of someone going out to negotiate a contract.

Jagan would have enjoyed his wife's company rather than his father's, but it would be unthinkable for women to sit with men, and Ambika had to keep her mother-in-law's company out of courtesy. It was a long seat running end to end below the windows. On Jagan's other side, there was a man from the forest with a string of beads around his neck, holding on his lap a small wooden cage containing a mottled bird, which occasionally let out a cry, sounding like doors moving on ancient unoiled hinges. When it made this noise, it drowned the conversation of the passengers (quite fifty of them in a vehicle expected to accommodate half that number legally, some with tickets, some without, for the conductor pocketed the cash and adjusted the records accordingly, for which purpose he was constantly pulling out a pad and making entries). Remarks, inquiries, advices, announcements, the babble of men's talk, women's shrill voices, and children's crying or laughing formed a perfect jumble and medley of sounds constantly overwhelmed by the shriek let out by the mottled bird. Jagan's father was engaged in a prolonged conversation with a peasant on his right, who was cracking groundnuts and littering the floor with shells, on the subject of manures and the technique of well-digging. Jagan glanced up at his wife and noticed that she was tired; the noise and the rattle were wearing her out. He wished he had her at his side. He would have pointed out and said, "See those trees, and those hills? Aren't they beautiful? Are you aware that this trip is for your benefit?" And she would probably have retorted, "For yours, let us say. I don't need a miracle to conceive. Remember the group photo in our house." And then he would have teased her, pinched her back, and so forth, which would have ended in a quarrel or in laughter. One couldn't say definitely. After all these years of married life, he could not really anticipate her reactions. Sometimes she took things easily, with the greatest cheer; sometimes she stung him and glared at him for the same remark. She was a model of goodness, courtesy, and cheerfulness generally, but she could lash with her tongue when her temper was roused.

A few weeks before, Father complained that something was wrong with the sauce; it turned out that it was over-salted. An on-the-spot inquiry was held. The mother-in-law demanded, "Amba, did you add salt to the sauce?" Amba said, "Yes, of course, Mother," in a polite tone from inside the kitchen. Mother was serving the men in the dining hall. At her daughter-in-law's admission, she dropped the plate in her hand and went in, demanding an explanation. "Who asked you to put salt into it?"

The girl replied haughtily, "I don't know," at which they heard the elder lady saying, "Should not a person have the sense to ask whether a thing is already salted or not? What's to happen when several hands add salt? The stuff is fit only for the street gutter, not for eating; this is how everything gets wasted and ruined in this house, I know. I know how it all happens. . . ."

"Bring some more rice," said Jagan's father from the dining hall. Ambika took the rice and served, leaving her mother-in-law to continue: "One doesn't ask for extraordinary things; they are not for us, we are not destined to enjoy the spectacle of a gold waist-band, like hundreds of others, but one wants at least a sensible—" She did not finish her sentence. Ambika was heard to cry, "I don't care," and, dropping the dish in her hand, she retired from the scene. She shut herself in her room and refused all food, throwing the whole house into a turmoil. She complained that she was not feeling like eating, that was all. Later in the week, when the situation had calmed down, she explained to Jagan, "Do you know what I said to your mother? 'Why are you so obsessed with the gold belt? What has it to do with salt or sugar? Have you never seen a gold belt in all your life?'" Since that day, his mother had been very sparing in her remarks, particularly with reference to the gold belt. They had all along underestimated Ambika's temper.

The bus deposited them in a village at the foot of the hill. It was probably the smallest village on any map, consisting of two rows of huts and a couple of wooden stands made of packing cases on which a little merchandise was displayed, mainly for the convenience of pilgrims going up-hill—coconuts, bananas, and betel leaves and flowers.

Mother was evidently tired after the journey and sat on a boulder to rest herself, while Father carried on interminable negotiations with the coconut-sellers over the price, trying to beat them down. Finally he yielded, grumbling that these villagers were spoilt nowadays and had become exploiters of the worst kind and flourishing his fists in anger. "We have come from the town twenty miles away. Should we not expect some consideration for our trouble?

"If I had known the price of things here, I'd have brought all the stuff from home," Father cried irascibly.

Mother interposed from where she sat, "That's not permitted. Custom requires . . ."

"Yes, yes, it was written in the Vedas ten thousand years ago that you must be exploited on this spot of earth by this particular coconut woman. True, true," he said cynically, glaring at his son and daughter-in-law sitting on another boulder, hinting that if only people displayed normal fecundity, one would not have to buy coconut at an exorbitant price. Jagan squirmed at the look his father gave him and felt more impotent than ever, and Ambika, at whom he glanced, looked more defiant than ever, ready to bring out the group photo of a hundred and three.

But for the fact that he was a coward, Jagan would have asked his parents, "Haven't you enough grandchildren? Why do you want more? Why don't you leave me alone?" Meanwhile the woman was saying, "Don't grudge a little extra expense, the grandson will bring you a lot of good fortune when he arrives." At which the old gentleman softened and asked, "How are you sure it'll be a son, not a daughter?" "No one who prays at that temple is ever disappointed with a daughter."

As if in fulfilment of the coconut-seller's prophecy, Mali was born. The very minute he was delivered (in the village home of his mother) he was weighed on a scale pan, even before the midwife could clean him up properly— and an equivalent weight in gold, silver, and corn was made up to be delivered to the God on Badri Hill, according to the solemn vow made during their visit.

When she came home, bringing the three-month-old baby, Ambika's parents sent with her an enormous load of gifts, as prescribed in the social code, for the first-born, and a huge feast was held for which a hundred guests were invited. The baby, passing from hand to hand, was crying, unable to bear the disturbance around him. The two grandfathers retired to a corner for a moment, leaving the other guests. "Mali," said one, "will have a deposit of a thousand rupees, earmarked, to which we will add a hundred on each birthday. This has been the practice in our family for generations whenever a child is born."

"So is it with us," said the other. "After all, we must provide for the new one and give him a good start in life."

"A new son in the house is a true treasure in this life and beyond life."

"I was dreading Jagan would be without issue," said Jagan's father.

"But I was in no doubt at any time. Barrenness is unknown in our house."

A look of triumph glowed on Jagan's face as he went from guest to guest, prostrated at their feet, and received blessings. Ambika followed him, prostrated at the feet of the guests, and was also blessed by everyone. She held herself up proudly, having now attained the proper status in the family. She looked especially gratified that she had enabled them to add, if it could somehow be done, one more figure to the group photographs hanging on the walls of both the houses.

Chapter Thirteen

Brooding on the past, Jagan must have dozed off at the foot of the statue. He was awakened by the clamour of birds alighting on the head of Sir F. Lawley. Jagan bestirred himself and looked at his house, now touched by the morning light, its heavy cornices emerging into view. "A little brighter now than at night," he said to himself, "but it has an unhappy look; it will never get back the light and laughter of other days. Who is there to brighten it? Not my son, nor his so-called—what do we call her, really? What name shall I give her? Anyway, where are they? Lost sight of. They don't come home. Where do they go? Never tell me. They are both alike. They are not the sort to make a home bright, unlike my mother or even Ambika when she was well. On the contrary, they blacken their surroundings. Probably they will be happier without me there."

Jagan felt it would be impossible for him to go back to that house. "It's tainted, but it is not my house that's tainted. It is his. Who am I to grumble and fret? I am sixty, and I may live for only ten or fifteen years more, whereas Mali, with or without his story machine, will have to go on for fifty years or more in that house. May he be blessed with longevity!" Jagan revelled for a moment in visions of Mali at eighty, and that profoundly moved his heart. But the immediate thought was: "Where will Grace be when Mali is eighty? Still in the same situation?" Perhaps Mali would succeed in sending her back. It was the best possible solution —if they still spurned his suggestion for a quick solemnization in the hills.

He felt hurt at the recollection as if a needle had probed a wound. "I have probably outlived my purpose in this house. If I live for ten or fifteen years more, it will have to be on a different plane. At sixty, one is reborn and enters a new janma." That was the reason why people celebrated their sixtieth birthdays. He remembered his father and mother, his uncle and aunt, and a score of other couples celebrating a man's sixtieth year like a wedding, with pipe, drum, and feasting. People loved to celebrate one thing or another all the time. He had had his fill of these festivals, and had nothing to complain of. Mali had proved that there was no need for ceremonials, not even the business of knotting the thali around the bride's neck. Nothing, no bonds or links or responsibility. Come together, live together, and kick each other away when it suited them. Whoever kicked harder got away first. Kick? Where was the kick? They sat in the green car with their legs intertwined in spite of what they had said of each other. Puzzling over things was enervating. Reading a sense into Mali's actions was fatiguing, like the attempt to spell out a message in a half-familiar script. He had no need to learn anything more. No more unravelling of conundrums, just as there was not going to be any more feasting or music in that shuttered house before him. When his sixtieth birthday came, it would pass unnoticed. A widower had no right to celebrate anything. He was fit only for retirement. What a magic word! If one had to shake things off, one did it unmistakably, completely, without leaving any loophole or a path back.

He still had to pay his visit to his house, to collect a few things he needed, though he would prefer to walk off, just walk off, as the Buddha did when he got enlightenment. It was five o'clock, his usual hour for the bath for half a century.

An hour later, after his morning ablutions and nourishment, he came out of his house carrying a little bundle, in which among other things was included his charka. "It's a duty I owe Mahatma Gandhi. I made a vow before him that I would spin every day of my life. I've got to do it, whether I'm at home or in a forest."

The sunlight, the cold bath, and the gruel he had had mitigated somewhat the ardour of his renunciation. He still had the key in his hand. "I must leave it somewhere," he thought, "with someone. I can't take it with me. . . ." But why not, after all?—it's the back-door key. The main key must be with Mali. If he never opens the door again, well, it's his business: it's his house that is going to become haunted with evil spirits, which might throw things about with a clatter." Jagan did not fully believe it, but he knew instances of deserted houses where such things happened. After all, evil spirits too needed accommodation somewhere. He chuckled at the thought of his inquiring, inquisitive neighbour. "Let him ask all the questions he likes of the ghost storming my house."

He still felt bothered about the key. "Why can't I leave it with my brother? It will be a good excuse to visit him." He toyed with the idea. Engage Gaffur's taxi, run to Vinayak Street, and leave the house key with his brother. Years ago, when he was chosen to take part in the National Struggle, he took elaborate leave of everyone before volunteering for arrest. His brother had tears in his eyes. The entire family were moved by his self-abnegation and accompanied him in a body halfway down the street, although they disapproved generally of his patriotic acts. He sighed for those warm and crowded days and longed for a similar send-off now. When they could show such intense feelings for a jail-going man, they might also display a little of it to a man retreating from life—even more so since this was going to be a kind of death actually. He'd breathe, watch, and occasionally keep in touch; but the withdrawal would not be different from death. He longed for a nice, crowded send-off now. But only his brother was left of an entire generation. He felt a longing for a glimpse of him. He had lost all his teeth, according to the cousin, and Jagan felt curious to know what he looked like now. He felt nostalgic for his brother's gruff voice uttering clipped sentences: ever a positive man and a born leader of younger brothers. The whole street was likely to crowd around Gaffur's taxi to look at one who was reputed to have become the father-in-law of a girl of outlandish origin. His brother would probably keep him standing in the street and tell him to throw the key from a distance for fear Jagan's shadow might taint the threshold. He might have to shout his explanation across, "I am off to a retreat. I'm sixty and in a new janma." He might have to speak about Mali too. "It's not only his marriage, but you must know the latest truth—that they are not married at all, but carry tales against each other, although they sit close in a motor car." And his brother might shout back, "Get away, you polluter of family reputations." And that crowd surrounding his taxi might jeer and laugh, obstruct his taxi, and force him to miss his bus at the Market Gate. Thus he would get caught again in the day's routine, and another day's and another day's. Impossible thought. "Better carry away the key. After all, it's the back door."

Passing Sir Frederick Lawley, he saw his cousin riding along clumsily on a bicycle, his tuft flying in the wind, his wheels zigzagging perilously onto the edge of the storm drain and retracting miraculously to the centre of the road. Jagan stood arrested by the spectacle; he had never seen the cousin on a bicycle before. The wheels seemed to come straight for him. Shouting incoherent inquiries, Jagan stepped aside. The cousin helplessly dashed past him a dozen yards and fell off the saddle, leaving the bicycle to bolt away by itself to a ditch. He picked himself up as Jagan got over his wonderment and demanded, "What is this circus feat so early in the day? At your age! You might kill yourself."

"Don't I know?" panted the cousin, dusting off the mud on the scratches at his elbow. "I was in a hurry to meet you, so I borrowed the bicycle from my neighbour. If you don't mind, I'll leave it in your house. I dare not ride it back."

Jagan said, "I have locked my house and am not going back." The unmistakable firmness of his tone made the cousin proceed straight to business. "Come with me. Our lawyer is waiting. Mali needs immediate help."

"Ah! What has happened?"

"Mali is in prison since last evening. . . ."

Jagan came to a dead stop on the road and screamed, "Oh God! Why?"

"He was found with half a bottle of alcohol in his car."

"Siva!" cried Jagan. "That's why I discouraged his idea of buying that horrible car!" He vented his rage against the green automobile until the cousin interrupted, "A bottle could be sneaked in anywhere. . . ."

"You don't understand. It's the motor car that creates all sorts of notions in a young fellow," said Jagan, and he found an agreeable escape into this theme. "Everything would have been well if he hadn't bought that car."

"Don't interrupt me, listen," said the cousin. "You must get him out of the police lock-up at once. It's not a good place to be in. We could have got him out last night, if you had not disappeared. Where were you?"

"I was only sleeping on the statue," Jagan said, and he remembered his wife's taunts whenever he proposed to sleep out.

"Fine time you chose to keep the statue company while I was searching for you everywhere!" exclaimed the cousin. "We could have got Mali out last night."

"Oh, what can we do now? Poor boy! In the lock-up! He won't feel comfortable; he has always slept on a spring mattress, since he was seven. How can I get him out?" Tears blurred his sight, until the cousin looked distorted, corrugated, and dwarfish.

The cousin watched him calmly and said, "Come, come. Don't let that vagrant see the tears in your eyes." The cousin was extremely practical and knew exactly what should be done. No wonder he was in such demand, thought Jagan, all over the town. Jagan asked, "Which lock-up?"

"In the sub-jail, until the trial begins. Get up, get up. Let us go and see if . . ."

Jagan felt giddy. He pressed his temples with his palms. "Don't pile on so much. I can't stand it." He felt faint and stretched himself flat at the foot of the statue.

The cousin said, "Let us go back to your house."

"No," said Jagan resolutely.

"You need rest. Don't worry. I will manage everything for you. . . ." The cousin patted his shoulder tenderly and said, "Don't lose nerve, what is all your philosophy worth if you cannot bear this little trial?"

"In the sub-jail . . . ," Jagan wailed. "I know the place; it is very dirty, prisoners urinate in a corner of the lock-up —or have they improved the conditions since my days?" he asked, blowing his nose.

"Naturally, it is all different now."

"Oh, yes, it must be different, I know, though so awful in those British days."

The cousin went on. "The first thing I did was to go out to the sub-jail and plead with the warders there. I saw the boy and spoke to him. I managed to get him a cup of coffee also."

"Did you give him anything to eat? He must have been hungry."

"They'll treat him specially. I know the District Collector, and so we can get things done. I got the news at six o'clock. I was returning from the house of the Superintending Engineer, where I had gone to fix up a home tutor for their son. At the turning near the General Post Office an orderly from the Superintendent's house gave me the news. The green car was halted at the Mempi outpost where they generally check for prohibition offences, as they find a lot of illicit distilling and traffic in the jungles high up. A policeman seems to have stopped Mali's car and found hidden in it half a bottle of some alcoholic drink, and you know how it is. . . . The police immediately seized the car, sealed the bottle before witnesses, and have charged the inmates of the car under the Prohibition Act."

"Who else was there?"

"Two of his friends."

"Oh, his friends have been his ruin. Where is the car now?"

"They drove it down. It will be kept at the police station till the case is finished."

Jagan sat up, shut his eyes, and remained silent, his lips moving in a prayer. "I . . . I didn't know the boy drank," he said, coming on a fresh discovery about his son.

"One doesn't have to drink to be caught by the Prohibition. It is enough if one's breath smells of alcohol. There are some fever mixtures which have an alcoholic flavour. A doctor has to certify that he had administered two doses of a fever mixture earlier in the day, that is all."

"Who would that doctor be?"

"Oh, you are wasting time. Come on, let us go," the cousin cried impatiently. "The lawyer will manage all that. Trust him and leave it in his hands. . . ."

"What was the green car doing on the hills?"

"That's beside the point. . . . Let's say Mali had gone up to confer with some parties on business, undisturbed, at the Peak House. He was expecting someone representing his foreign collaborators."

Jagan recovered his composure. "Ah, foreign collaborators! Impressive word. No one in India knows about business. Always foreign! Well, accepted, sir. But the bottle? How did it get in?"

"Someone left it there. A stranger stopped the car on the mountain road, asked for a lift, got off on the way, and perhaps left the bottle behind." Jagan felt partly relieved at such possibilities. He studied his cousin's face to judge the quantum of truth in his explanations, but that man avoided his eyes, and said generally, "Anything is possible these days. You can't trust people, especially strangers. When I didn't find you in, I went in search of Ganesh Rau, our lawyer, the best in our district. Though he is up to his neck in work, he has accepted our case: he knows Mali and admires his plans. He seems to have promised to buy shares in Mali's company when the time comes."

"Does he believe Mali's machine can write stories?"

"I had no time to discuss all that, but he said, 'Why not?' when I mentioned it."

Jagan became reflective. The cousin said, "All that apart, the case is very strongly in our favour. We sat discussing all the possibilities until two o'clock in the morning. I could find no time for sleep at all. At five o'clock I borrowed the bicycle and fell off it four times before reaching you."

"Don't go on a bicycle again. You might kill yourself," said Jagan pontifically.

The cousin said, "He is also looking into the antecedents of the policeman who checked Mali's car at the outpost. That stranger who accosted them could have been the policeman's accomplice. They may have had a grudge against you."

"Why?" asked Jagan. "Why should any policeman bear any grudge against me?"

"For a hundred reasons," said the cousin. "People are generally bad. He might have been demanding free packets of sweets from your shop; after all, poor fellows, they are so ill paid that they do seek favours from shop men. You might not remember it now; but you will have to try and recollect how you threatened to report him to his officers."

"I have never seen a policeman in my shop. . . ."

"Or he might have marked you that time years ago when you violated the laws. . . ."

Jagan laughed at this idea. "If a grudge was to be borne, we had greater cause than the police."

"Very well, it could be so. . . ."

"But Mahatma Gandhi trained us not to nurse any resentment. . . . Anyway, the policemen of our days must all be senile or dead now."

"Or he might have had a brush with Mali sometime. Policemen are generally prejudiced against young people driving scooters or cars, you know. This is all just casual talk, that's all; the lawyer will instruct you what to say. We should depend upon his guidance. One thing is certain. Just answer his cross-examination as he directs you. The whole issue will turn on your evidence."

Jagan said briefly, "If what you say is true, well, truth will win. If it is not true, there is nothing I can do."

"No, no, don't say so. We must do our best to get Mali out. They could sentence him up to two years under this act."

"Who are we to get him out or to put him in?" asked Jagan philosophically. He had recovered from the first shock totally, and spoke even impishly now, although his voice was still a little thick with grief. "Truth ought to get him out, if what you say is true," he repeated.

"But the lawyer will have to build it up and establish it," said the cousin, "with proper evidence. He is thinking of ways and means. If he is able to establish the malafides of the policeman, we may even file a counter case in order to strengthen ours."

Jagan's mind had attained extraordinary clarity now. He threw a look at his bag, lightly lifted it, and said, "I wish you all luck; you and your lawyer and his distinguished client and also that poor soul—the policeman who had the misfortune to stop the green car: but don't expect me to take any part in it. Leave me out of it completely; forget me and I'll go away without asking too many questions."

"Where, where are you going?" asked the cousin anxiously.

"I will seek a new interest—different from the set of repetitions performed for sixty years. I am going somewhere, not carrying more than what my shoulder can bear. All that I need is in that bag. . . ."

"Including the bank book, I suppose," asked the cousin, "which is a compact way of carrying things. How far are you going?"

Jagan described the retreat across the river. The cousin was aghast. "I know that place near the cremation ground.

179

Has that hair-dyer been trying to sell it to you? Forgive me if I say, 'Keep away from him.' He is a sorcerer: knows black magic and offers to transmute base metals into gold. . . ."

"I don't care what he does. I am going to watch a Goddess come out of a stone. If I don't like the place, I will go away somewhere else. I am a free man. I've never felt more determined in my life. I'm happy to have met you now, but I'd have gone away in any case. Everything can go on with or without me. The world doesn't collapse even when a great figure is assassinated or dies of heart failure. Think that my heart has failed, that's all."

He gave the cousin a bunch of keys and said, "Open the shop at the usual hour and run it. Mali will take charge of it eventually. Keep Sivaraman and the rest happy; don't throw them out. You can always come over to the retreat if there is anything urgent, or to render an account. I'll tell you what to do. At the Market Gate buses leave for Mempi every four hours starting from eight-thirty in the morning. You are a busy man, but please help me now."

"Yes, I'll do anything you say," said the cousin, rather intimidated by Jagan's tone. "The lawyer wanted two thousand rupees for preliminary expenses. He will arrange the bail. Mali should be out before this evening."

"A dose of prison life is not a bad thing. It may be just what he needs now," said Jagan, opening his bag and taking out his cheque-book. Resting it on his knee, he wrote out a cheque and handed it to the cousin.

"If there are further charges?" asked the cousin.

"We'll pay them, that is all. You can ask me whenever you like. I am not flying away to another planet."

The cousin was amazed at the transformation in Jagan, who kept repeating, his eyes still wet, "A little prison life won't harm anyone. I must not miss the eight-thirty bus at

Market Gate. I don't want to ask questions, but tell me where is she?" he asked, rising and shouldering his bag.

"She has friends who have found a job for her in a women's hostel . . ." the cousin began.

But Jagan dismissed the subject halfway through the other's explanation. "If you meet her, tell her that if she ever wants to go back to her country, I will buy her a ticket. It's a duty we owe her. She was a good girl."

GLOSSARY

Almirah: A cupboard.

Bonda: A savoury dish made of flour and fried in oil.

Charka: A hand-operated spinning wheel.

Dhoti: A sarong-like article of men's wear, tucked and knotted at the waist.

Dosai: A fried cake made of rice paste.

Jaggery: A product similar to brown sugar, made by boiling sugar-cane juice.

Janma: A rebirth.

Jibba: A loose, long shirt buttoned at the shoulder.

Jilebi: A sweet made of corn and flour.

Jutka: A two-wheeled carriage.

Khaddar: Hand-spun yarn and cloth woven from it.

Lakh: A hundred thousand.

Paisa (plural *Paise*): The smallest coinage; one hundred paise make a rupee, which is the equivalent of 7.5 cents at the present rate of exchange.

Puja: Worship, offering.

Pyol: A platform, for sitting, built along a house wall that faces the street.

Sait: A suffix to certain classes of northern Indian names, generally applied in the South to businessmen from the North.

Satyagraha: Gandhi's doctrine of tolerance and nonviolence.

Seer: A unit of measure equal to slightly over two pounds.

Shastras: Scriptures laying down rules of conduct, etc.

Sohan Papdi: A very elegant sweetmeat made of melted sugar candy, flavoured with saffron, and dressed with nuts of all kinds.

Thali: A yellow thread knotted around the bride's neck by the bridegroom at the auspicious moment they become man and wife; it remains around the wife's neck for the rest of her life.

Tulasi: A tiny sacred plant grown and nurtured in the courtyard of every home; it is considered to be a goddess in this form and is worshipped at the dawn of each day by the women of the house.

Uppamav: A dish made of boiled rice.

Viswarupa: A vision of God in his full stature, filling and enveloping the whole universe.